THE UNBROKEN ROSE

CHRISTINA C JONES

2020.

What a year, right?

So much to mourn, but maybe, hopefully, a few things also to celebrate.
Dacia's story was difficult to tell - not because of her, because of me.
Could I put myself aside to give her the happy ending she deserved?
Well, I sure tried.
Thank you, to all the usual suspects. We've been doing this for years now -
you know who you are, and you know what you mean to me.
Always.
-CCJ

ABOUT

Broken.

A word typically ascribed to fragmented, useless things – not people.

A word most would easily impose upon a woman like Dacia, knowing she's been through the kind of things that are *meant* to leave a person fragmented.

A word that comes with pre-conceived notions, judgements… limitations.

None of which she embraces, or accepts.

Because what if putting the pieces back together is the very thing that makes her stronger?

one

I WAS BEING FOLLOWED.

For days now, if not *weeks*.

Definitely days.

For that long, I'd been certain.

It was always at a distance, never close enough that the average person would even notice, most likely. That meant they were good at it, which was worrisome.

The thing was, I wasn't the average woman - maybe they knew that, maybe they didn't.

If they *didn't* know, that was a good thing. For me, at least. Maybe not for them. But if they *did*, and followed me anyway, well... *let's just hope they didn't.*

The soles of my athletic shoes made a steady *tap, tap, tap,* against the pavement as I trotted up the half-lit sidewalk, not wanting to break my pace. I was tired, and really should've been winding down from my too-early in the morning meditation session.

That's what this was for me - supposed to be something peaceful, a way to clear my mind. But now I was on edge, because someone had interrupted my serenity.

Just the thought of it made me angry, because... how dare they?

I didn't cross anyone, didn't mess with anybody.

I minded my business, just lived my life.

All I wanted was solitude - to be left alone and not reminded of what my life used to be, so I could remain firmly planted in what it was *now*.

I just... I wouldn't live like that anymore.

Nope.

Today, whatever this was, was about to stop.

This is a terrible idea, a little voice in my head popped up, as I suddenly rounded into an alley that was definitely not on my plan. I pushed that to the back of my mind though, forcing myself to regulate my breathing as I pulled my body into a fighting stance.

At first, it was quiet except for the music still playing in one ear. The *street* was quiet, the residential area tucked far enough away from the glitz and glam of what most attributed to Vegas to be polluted by the constant traffic and noise.

Gently, I pulled the other bud from my ear, tucking it into the relative safety of my sports bra. Once I'd done that, the steady patter of the other runner's shoes coming up the pavement was clear as a bell.

Maybe it was a coincidence.

Maybe this was just someone else who'd taken to using the quiet of early morning as their personal sanctuary, like I had. As the footsteps drew closer, I doubted myself, wondering if I was just being paranoid.

God knows I had plenty of reason for that.

But as the time ticked down for me to either act or let them pass, I remembered the admonition I'd received from the wisest person I knew.

If you feel like something isn't right, trust it.

I didn't trust *this*.

Not at all.

Because of that, it took little for me to draw on the strength of pure adrenaline, timing myself to put my full power into a high kick just as the other runner was passing the alley.

I felt connected, but whoever was on the receiving end absorbed the blow like it was nothing, grabbing my thigh to take away my momentum.

Okay.

Fine.

Instead of relying on the more prevalent strength of my legs, I used my fists, raining blows wherever I could land them even though I could barely see my dark-clad attacker in the dark. There was too much going on - too much blood rushing through my ears, too much fear coursing through my veins.

I could hear myself being told to stop, but I wouldn't.

Ever.

If I had to die right here on the street, so be it, but I would give every ounce of strength in my body towards the cause of not being taken.

Never again.

"Dacia!"

The sound of my name on my assailant's lips cut right through all the chaos of the moment. Now, icy fear crept up my spine as I realized this was absolutely a worst-case scenario.

Strong hands gripped my wrists, easily pinning them together while they pushed me out to be held at a distance.

"Dacia, *stop it*. It's me."

I blew out a stream of air, trying to clear the hair from my face so I can see who "me" was. I wasn't even sure how the puff I'd secured it into this morning had come undone, but it took a helping hand from my captor to push the wild coils out of my eyes so I could see into his.

Familiar hazel orbs I never expected to gaze upon again.

Vaguely hoped?

Sure.

But never *expected*.

"*Zay.*"

When I spoke his name aloud, that must have triggered

something for him. He let me go, dropping my wrists from his hold as his full lips spreading to show perfect white teeth that make the whole visual rather dazzling.

Dizzying.

But I still found the gumption—the *anger* - to form two fists and launch at him again.

"What the fuck is wrong with you?!" I demanded, completely unamused as he caught my arms again, laughing. "You scared the shit out of me!"

He was still grinning as I snatched away.

"I'm sorry. Seriously," he insisted. "I wasn't trying to scare you. I really didn't expect you to notice I was here."

"*You* taught me to notice," I reminded him.

Reminded *myself.*

Probably not the best idea, because having him in front of me, remembering things, was making me... well... *remember things.*

Things I would much rather stay buried.

"So you didn't forget everything I taught you, huh?" he teased, keeping a fair distance from me, probably in case I tried to attack him again.

The benefit of that was being able to really get a good look at him, to see how the slender, sinewy body he'd walked around in last time I laid eyes on him had given away to the thicker, muscled frame of a fully grown man.

A thorn.

A *killer.*

Shaking my head, I turned my attention somewhere else, toward the steadily growing band of orange across the sky marking the true start of the day.

"What are you doing here?" I asked.

"What do you *think* I'm doing here, Dee?"

The teenaged heart still buried somewhere deep in me said one thing, but my adult, real world logic said something else.

"How the hell am I supposed to know?"

He stared for a moment, completely still, as if he knew he was about to say something that might disappoint me.

"Protection detail."

Oh.

Not exactly what I wanted to hear, but not remotely surprising.

"So what… you work for my sister now?" I asked, crossing my arms. Then, I moved my hands up to fix my ponytail. Propped my hands on his hips. I couldn't stay still.

Isaiah—his full name, maybe—smirked. "I prefer to think of myself as a private contractor."

"Yeah, I'm sure you do."

"What does that mean?"

"It doesn't mean anything Zay - I'm just talking, because I don't know what else to do. I didn't… I didn't know what happened to you. How long has it been?"

I knew the answer to that, maybe, but he most likely didn't. The passage of time in the Garden was always fuzzy. My memories of it were all exacerbated by deeper horrors than some others had to endure.

But I remembered being young and impatient, and wanting more from him than he could give me—because of rules, and maybe unreciprocated feelings.

I wasn't sure.

"I don't know," he admitted. "Probably… seven or eight years?"

"*Before* everything… went down."

Before the Garden fell.

"Yeah," he nodded, that smile of his taking on a wistful slant that made my chest ache. "All of that was pretty crazy, huh? Worked out for you, though. I know you always wanted a sister."

"Before I knew how much of a pain in my ass she was

going to be," I replied, trying to keep some levity in a conversation that left no room for it.

Not with *this* subject.

Zay shook his head. "You say that, but it's probably good for you. The position you're in now... this suits you. You always seemed like a bit of a princess, so it's no big surprise to find out you damn near *are* one."

He didn't mean that as an insult, I didn't think.

But it damn sure felt like one.

Especially considering that until recently, my life hadn't exactly been what one would consider *charmed*.

"Should I be thanking you for that statement, or...?"

"It's not... I didn't mean it like that. I'm just saying," he shrugged. "With everything you went through, you deserve to live like you are now."

Instant moisture sprang to my eyes, immune to my attempts to blink it away as he kept talking.

"I didn't know what had happened—what was going on. If I did, I would've..."

I gave him a wry smile, glad he hadn't found the words to finish that statement. Thinking about all the times the memory of him had drifted in and out of my conscious, all the times I'd prayed and dreamed for him to come for me, to *save* me...

Well, that hurt bad enough.

I didn't need to hear it.

"I know," I told him. "It doesn't matter anyway though. Not anymore."

"It matters to me that you know I would've done something, if I'd known."

"I said I know."

It was quiet between us again then, for several long seconds, making it hard to stand still.

Again.

"I'm gonna finish my run," I said, and then took off

without warning. I didn't look back to see if he was following— of course he was following, if he was supposed to be my "protection detail".

Something I'd already told Alicia I didn't need.

To her credit, she'd never agreed to that.

Like Isaiah, she hadn't known about the very private hell I'd gone through—something deeper, cruder, than the typical commitment of a Thorn or Rose. Not that *that* was desirable either, but it was... bearable.

What wasn't tolerable was what had come after I was taken from the Garden, before I was pulled from the clasp of even *deeper* wickedness. The in-between time, *that* was the source of all my nightmares. The parts I could remember were ugly and terrifying. And the thought of what I *couldn't* remember... well, that was even scarier.

I'd been used as currency, as a cheap toy, as a vessel for... the worst things I didn't have to imagine.

I didn't *want* to remember.

I wanted to look forward and *never* have to look backward again.

Alicia wanted that too.

Insisted on it, actually, as much as she could.

My head was too fucked up to understand the gravity of it at the time, but now? Knowing what she'd taken on for my sake - mentally, emotionally, *physically*—to destroy the nerve center of so much of our pain...

Fine.

I wouldn't make a fuss about the protection.

As much as I didn't want to need it, she was probably right.

More and more, the story of the *long-lost Pelletier sisters* was a source of interest, which meant—to our chagrin—more and more eyes.

More attention.

More vulnerability.

And my penchant for running in the dark was probably not the wisest thing in the world.

So I got it.

It didn't take me long to get home—now that I knew exactly who was following me, there was no true rhyme or reason to variating my path. If a Thorn decided he was coming into my home, there was extraordinarily little that would stop him.

And there was nothing *I* would do to stop *this* one.

In fact, he stopped himself, hesitating at the door of my cozy little house tucked into the Las Vegas hills. "Are you going to tell Alicia that you caught me?" he asked, barely out of breath as I bent over, panting before I keyed in the code that allowed access to my lock, then pulled the key from around my neck.

"How else would I pick a fight with her over hiring security without telling me?" I asked, stepping into the soothing, temperature-controlled oasis of my foyer. "You coming in?"

His gaze dropped from my face to my body, settling on my breasts, the juncture of my thighs, and then back to my face. "I shouldn't. I've already fucked up my bonus now that you've seen me."

"What does that have to do with you coming inside?"

A smirk spread over his lips, and he raised a finger to scratch at a scar bisecting his eyebrow and cheek—something he didn't have when I knew him before. "Well… I have explicit instructions on how I'm supposed to engage you. And… how I'm *not*."

"Meaning… what?" I asked, leaning into the doorframe.

"Meaning… I'm not supposed to fuck you."

My eyebrow shot up. "And that's what you think is gonna happen if you come in?"

"I think we probably shouldn't take that chance, should we?"

I returned his smirk and closed the door, even though…
that wasn't what I wanted.

I wished I had a witty remark, some seductive words, or
even… hell, *anger* would've been better.

Would've been… more.

There was no way Alicia knew my history with Zay, or she
wouldn't have hired him.

Of all the men who'd hurt me in one way or another… he
may have cut me deepest.

OFTEN, I couldn't sleep.

In those times, I would turn to the power of melatonin—maybe it was some placebo effect, maybe not. All I knew was that for me, it worked.

The horrifically lurid dreams were an unfortunate side effect.

And so, night after night, I would find myself up later than recommended, weighing the benefits of sleep against the chance of reliving the worst dredges of my memories via nightmare.

Some nights I chose wrong.

I woke up in a cold sweat, with Isaiah's name on my lips. Not for the first time, not by a long shot. Only now, instead of the boyishly handsome face of a barely twenty-year-old, my mind's eye had replaced his features with the rugged jawline, battle scars, and enigmatic gaze of a grown man who'd seen—and maybe *done*—the unfathomable.

Isaiah as he was *now*.

A small comfort.

A glance at the time told me it was painfully early, but I rolled myself out of bed anyway, trekking to my tiny kitchen for a glass of water.

To soothe my throat *and* my nerves.

Maxim Bisset and Sebastian Gray—dead men who didn't

deserve the honor of my sub-conscious attention—had held starring roles in tonight's dreams. I'd grown proficient enough at stifling the trauma when I was awake, but my nightmares were a stronghold I couldn't suppress into complete defeat.

They hadn't defeated *me* either though.

Neither the dreams nor the reality had left me as ruined as the intent had so been.

Back in my room, my cell phone screen was lit with notifications of varying importance. The one I focused on for now was from Alicia, inviting me to the gym at her compound for a sparring session.

Of course I wasn't about to turn *that* down.

As stifling as her attention could be, as overprotective as she was, I was fascinated by Alicia—and still a little terrified, which I'd never admit to anyone. When the Garden fell—when *she* felled the Garden, in pursuit of me—I'd barely even been able to look at her. They'd done something to me, trained my brain to associate her face with trauma, and pain, and fear. A sick compliment to the suppression of my identity.

Stuff the memories in a box, guard the box with triggers.

It had worked remarkably well until it didn't.

Yes, her presence had made it feel like I was dying, and *no*, I couldn't remember her, but… she was mine, and I was hers. I couldn't shake the painful truth of that, couldn't let it go.

And now, years later, I was embarrassed by my reaction to her.

Learning what *her* journey had been, the lengths she'd gone to find me, the sacrifices she'd been willing to make… only for me to reject her.

Yeah.

I didn't turn down invites.

She was an early bird like me, so I wasn't surprised by the early hour she'd listed in her text. Actually, I would have to get moving to make it to her place on time, so that's what I did.

I only wondered briefly if Zay was following me here, and then pushed it from my mind. Alicia would notice immediately if I were distracted—she always did—and I wasn't prepared to talk to her about him. I hadn't even said anything yet about knowing she'd hired protection against my wishes for exactly that reason.

I wasn't sure I could explain it if I tried.

So I wouldn't.

"Good morning—how's the arm today?" Alicia asked, looking up as I walked through the door of the gym room. There was a bigger area downstairs, that the former Roses and Thorns she'd collected used for group training, but this one was private.

Quiet.

"It's okay," I assured her, my fingers instinctively going to the troublesome spot. Three years ago, a gunshot wound had ripped my flesh apart, but physical therapy had done wonders. I'd kept most feeling and mobility, but the area remained sensitive—*hypersensitive* sometimes.

Our last sparring match had been one of those times, the nagging sensation of pins and needles making it hard for me to focus *and* perform. I was no quitter though, so I'd been giving the exercise everything I had.

Until Alicia got me with a jab dead in the middle of the problematic spot.

I'd passed out from the pain.

I was here now though, and ready to give it another shot—with Alicia's assurance that she would avoid hitting me there again.

"So talk to me about Isaiah," she said, moving into a fighting stance, and waiting for me to join.

Oh.

She was hitting me *here* instead.

"What makes you think there's something to talk about?" I asked as I moved to face her.

"The fact that you haven't fussed at me for hiring him," she smirked. "Nothing I found in his history—or from what he told me—suggested that the two of you might know each other. And yet... clearly you do."

I raised an eyebrow, dropping my hands to my sides. "*Clearly*? That's a reach."

"But is it wrong?"

I cast my gaze up to the ceiling, cursing myself for taking what should have been obvious bait. "No."

"Thought so. Okay," she mused, sauntering up to where I stood. "If you hated him, you would've been in my face about it as soon as you found out, so it's something else then. What was it? A fling or something?"

"There was no *fling*. It was... a crush."

Alicia's raised eyebrow said a lot more about her disbelief than her mouth did. But that really was the way the story had gone.

I was an overzealous teenager, with an inappropriate obsession with the Thorn tasked to protect me.

Reciprocated feelings?

Of course not.

That wasn't the Thorn—or Rose—way.

This was my sister though. And the whole thing with Zay had happened nearly a decade ago. And the Garden didn't exist anymore.

It wasn't like telling the truth would get us in "trouble".

But... getting "in trouble" wasn't the only consideration here. I didn't particularly care to dredge up painful memories of having and then abruptly, brutally, losing something that had felt so incredibly sacred.

"So... you were in love with him?" Alicia correctly

surmised. There was no flippancy in her tone—no minimalization. "How long ago?"

I shook my head, finally *really* returning my gaze to hers. I'd been avoiding her eyes, but I met them now, knowing there was no getting around this conversation. "A decade, probably. We were kids. *I* was a kid. He was a little older."

"When you say kids…?"

"Pen's age," I clarified, referring to another rescued Rose. "I was seventeen. He'd just gotten his mark, so… nineteen. Maybe twenty."

"Too old for you."

I rolled my eyes. "In a normal world, probably. Nothing ever happened anyway."

"You were in love with him though."

"Nothing *physical* happened, I mean. We… couldn't have. And he wouldn't have."

Alicia nodded. There was no need for me to explain to her the rules that would have been in place, barring intimacy between us. Truly unbreakable ones, in absence of a death wish, which neither of us had.

Not then.

"So… you're telling me that the rogue Thorn I hired to follow your stubborn ass, thinking you wouldn't catch on because he wasn't a familiar face… was what… your first love or something?"

Only.

She was trying to talk to me like we were normal, which I appreciated, but was completely dissonant from reality. Her path had differed completely from mine, even though we'd come from the same place, and still… she had *one* love, which was all people like us were afforded.

If we got it at all.

Just Cree.

I shrugged, fidgeting with the straps of my padded sparring

gloves. "I guess you could put it like that. But it was a decade ago, and like I said… we were kids. It doesn't matter."

"But you didn't say anything to me about it. You would've said something if it didn't matter."

I smirked.

Damn.

Was I really *that* easy to read?

I wanted to tell myself it was less about me, more about the fact that she'd been a Rose too—the dangerous kind. Perception and profiling were engrained in her, skills imprinted into the core of who she was.

Of course she could tell.

"Maybe I'm not saying anything because it *shouldn't* matter."

She raised an eyebrow at me. "Maybe you trying to convince me it shouldn't matter is prime evidence that it definitely should. That it *does.*"

"Too much has happened since then."

"And what exactly does any of it have to do with right now?"

Frustrated, I shook my head, turning to walk away from her. "Do I really have to explain this to you?"

"No, you don't *have* to, but if you don't, I'll be in the dark. Because—*despite* my other objections with the possibility of what we're discussing here—I *don't* see what's stopping two free adults from… doing whatever the hell you want."

I pushed out a sigh, stopping at the rack that held the weights and other equipment. "He told me it was all in my head, okay? An… unrequited crush."

"Well, of course he did," Alicia scoffed. "From what you told me, you'd been given a special status because of your moth—because of Paloma," she corrected herself. "I'm sure he wasn't supposed to touch you."

"Right. But… what I'm telling you is, it wasn't *just* about us not getting in trouble. We never got into trouble, were never questioned, none of that. He just… changed one day. No more laughing, talking, and when I asked him about it, he… acted like I was crazy. Like I was making things between us out to be something they weren't. And then, not long after… he was gone."

Alicia's lips parted, but she said nothing. Still, there was understanding in her eyes as she nodded. "He broke your heart."

"Yeah."

Before I even knew what that was, when I didn't have anybody else, that rejection had… shattered me.

"If he'd just gotten his ink, he was probably about to be sent out for field work. And… Dosh, you know how it goes— no personal attachments. No liabilities. He did it because he had to."

"*Or* that was just his truth," I shrugged. "And if that was his truth then, *surely* now that I've… nevermind. It just doesn't matter anymore. Period."

Her eyebrows went up. "So, conversation over then? No room for me to push back on your unspoken assertion that somehow you might not deserve his returned affection anymore, because of something done to you? I don't get to tell you how ridiculous that is?"

"Yes, yes, and no," I answered with a pointed glare. "I didn't want to talk about any of this, remember? I thought we were sparring?"

"Aren't we doing that right now, little sister?"

I rolled my eyes at her attempted humor—my chest was too tight, face too hot about the subject to joke over it. Which was embarrassing in and of itself, because no matter what other variables came into play, the *fact* remained that I was still flustered over a—possibly—unreciprocated crush from a decade ago.

It was pitiful.

Before I could reply—and keep this wonderful conversation going—the door to the gym room opened and Yaya, Alicia's daughter, came toddling in, as fast as her little feet could carry her. She was closely followed by her father. Their energy brought an immediate, pleasant shift in energy.

I'd never been more glad to have Yaya's little hands reaching up at me.

"Hi Dee-Deeeee," she sang at me, squealing as I tickled under her chin. "You're fighting with my 'Lesha?"

"Not in the way you think, lil' bit," I told her, shooting a glance at my sister, and Cree, who stood beside her. "We were just finishing a conversation, but I think we're done, which means you can help me find a pancake somewhere in this house, right?"

Yaya was incredulous, her teensy eyebrows folding together in a frown. "I dunno. Daddy said maybe cereal."

I let out a fake gasp. "I think Daddy just didn't feel like making them," I said, with a teasing smile at Cree. "But that's what Dee-Dees are for!"

"Okay!" was her cheerful response, and I used her enthusiasm as my cover to get the hell out of there, away from this dialogue I didn't care to have.

I'd much rather spend my morning loving on my niece.

Three

A YEAR OR SO AGO, I messed up.

And honestly, *I messed up* was putting it mildly.

See, I was going to therapy, like I was supposed to, and one thing the therapist kept mentioning was that it seemed like there was something I was still bottling inside me.

Because... of course there was.

I couldn't exactly tell her about the Garden. About being abducted as a child, having my memories stripped from me, being trained as a Rose who specialized in the perverse pleasures of men.

And I *really* couldn't explain being abducted from *that* version of hell only to be immersed in one that was even more horrific - no need for me to be lucid, willing, or hell... even upright.

All my therapist knew was... sex trafficking.

And she also knew that no amount of whatever tools she had in her arsenal would get me to talk through the details of that with her, so she'd encouraged me to write it out.

Not like an assignment to turn in, but something just for me. It could be journal entries, diary, or fictionalization, whatever I wanted it to be. As long as I got some of the noise out of my head, and onto metaphorical paper, so that my thoughts were no longer so disjointed.

That fragmentation had made the triggers so much easier

to run into, that merging them for my mental health was a no-brainer.

So I wrote.

Not with paper and pen, but with my laptop and keys.

At first, it was all just a step above gibberish, but eventually it started coming together.

There was a story there.

A scared little girl, the big sister who tried her best to be strong, but she was just a kid too. The trauma of seeing their father killed in front of them, being taken, separated, made to forget each other.

Being reprogrammed to something intended only as a product, to fulfill a service to a customer.

The tough sister used as a killer, the weak sister used as a pet.

And then, realizing that even in that life where she wasn't free, that the little girl—not so little anymore - was privileged. She received specific protection most of the others didn't get.

Eventually she would know that was simply a monster's attempt at feigning motherly care, but in the meantime it was accepted as normal.

Until she was taken to be used again.

As a method of revenge - a bargaining chip.

Resigned to an inevitable, sad death, and maybe even prepared to do it herself.

Until her sister came to rescue her.

I labored over it for weeks, barely sleeping, barely eating, just needing to get it all down.

Out.

Once I finally came out of that frantic state, once I'd read it all back and re-experienced all the horror... I convinced myself that the world needed to see it.

It wasn't just *my* story, it was the story of many dozens of others.

Maybe someone would see it and know they weren't as alone in the world as they might feel.

So... I put it on a fiction site, and then, finally, I slept.

I played with my niece, and had meals with sister and Pen, and I talked to Tempest -another former Rose - on the phone. And I just... *lived*.

Basking in the weight off my shoulders.

Until finally, after about a week, I went back to it.

People had seen it.

People had *read* it.

People had... loved it, and insisted they wanted to see the story brought to life, complete with all the heroes and villains, on their screens.

So I deleted it.

Because it wasn't just... *some story*, it was my life. And like I'd used as a selling point for my recklessness—not *only* mine.

How incredibly *stupid.*

It wasn't like many people had seen it - not on some random fiction site consisting mostly of angst-ridden love stories about teenagers. I could see that it had only gathered a couple hundred views before I deleted it.

But still.

That was dumb.

Only one person—Tempest - knew I'd done that, and even her knowledge of it was purely random. I kept it to myself, because nobody else *needed* to know how utterly careless I'd been, in that moment of madness.

But.

As reckless as it had been, there was no denying how having something like that to focus on, being able to pour those things onto a page and get them out of my head, had been incredibly cathartic.

So I tried it again.

Not with my *own* story this time, with a story belonging to one of the other characters in my head. I'd spent enough time lonely, watching the whims and whimsies of others, I'd traveled enough, seen enough that I had the lived experience to make my imagination incredibly vivid.

It was also a little cruel.

Despite the complete opposite of a fairy tale life I lived for myself, that seemed to be what my brain favored in fiction. Sweet, warm, fuzzy, so saccharine they made your teeth hurt stories was what I specialized in.

Under a pen name.

My therapist *knew* about that, but no one else did.

"Whatever it takes for you to be okay," she'd said, thrilled that I'd found some outlet. I was sure that eventually I'd get challenged on it, forced to explore why the content of what I wrote was what it was.

But in the meantime, I just wanted to bask in it.

These stories where these people got to just be *happy*. They didn't have to walk through holy fire to prove they deserved it, didn't have to be broken and bleeding first.

They were simply happy because they *were*, and what a concept that was to me.

Not that I was *un*happy - there were definitely things that brought me joy - but mostly I was just… here.

My ignored computer screen suddenly went to sleep, bathing the room in darkness. That got my attention, and I moved my mouse to wake everything back up, returning my gaze to what I've been looking at before my thoughts had gotten away from me.

I was supposed to be booking a writing retreat.

Escape was a Whitfield property recently opened in Southern California. An exclusive luxury resort with private beaches and villas over saltwater lagoons. The pictures were amazing, so peaceful-looking that I wished I could just blink myself there.

Of course, I could just hop on a quick flight… if I wanted everybody in my business.

Alternatively, it was only six-and-a-half-hour drive. I could use that time of complete solitude to let whatever ideas I was taking with me marinade.

I did not have to think it over very long.

I had the reservation all set up anyway from when I was just dreaming about it, so I clicked submit. A moment later, I was rewarded with a congratulatory message on a pop up from the site.

I *needed* this getaway.

Needed the absolute lack of interruptions, needed nobody checking in with me, needed to see something other than Vegas every damn day. This was one benefit of having inherited a massive family fortune—getting to use it for moments exactly like this.

I went to my email to double-check my booking information. Soon I was going to have to get my ass up and start packing for the trip I was apparently embarking on the very next day. For the moment, I took the time to glance at what other messages I might have, knowing that I was going to be unavailable for the next few days.

A new message in my inbox from Rowan Phillips at the Cartwright center made my heart race. I didn't even know what it said, yet just knowing it was there, waiting, made me nervous.

Cree had grown up with Rowan in the local foster care system and worked with her in various charity endeavors. Her center had made huge strides for the underserved communities nearby. It was the pinnacle of what people meant when they talked about wanting to see privileged people put their money where their mouths were when they claimed to want to "give back".

So what better person to help me with my own endeavor,

using some of my inheritance, to create a resource for other people - adults and children alike—who'd suffered through the indignity and terror of sex trafficking.

I couldn't open it right now.

Because if I did, I would spend the bulk of what was supposed to be a relaxing getaway planning and strategizing instead. I closed the lid on the laptop, leaving it where it was for when I packed *that* bag later.

For now, I focused on the clothes.

Bathing suits and maxi dresses were all I needed—I had no plans to give any more thought than absolutely necessary to what I was putting on from day to day for the time I was there. I just wanted to be comfortable. At the last moment, I shoved a few pairs of shorts and a couple tee shirts in my bag, all the way at the bottom.

I would do my level best to *not* need them.

I got my toiletries together, underwear, all that, then ran through a mental checklist of anything else I might need. I kept my car gassed and had enough snacks already stocked in my house that I could put some things together for the road without having to stop.

This was going to be *lovely*.

———

I FROWNED at the sound of my doorbell.

It was too early in the morning for unexpected visitors, and nobody had called or texted me about stopping by.

I put down the bags I'd been about to take through the garage door to load the car, a deep feeling of dread in the pit of my stomach as I headed to answer the front door.

None of the possibilities in my mind were good.

Had something happened? Was someone hurt?

Those were the genuine emergencies that made me not

drag my feet to answer, even though the third possibility had me tempted to make a run for it instead.

Maybe someone knew about my trip.

I had said nothing, but spyware on my computer—or someone monitoring my email—weren't outside the realm of possibility. Alicia still worked as Kingston Whitfield's head of security, and it wouldn't surprise me at all if me booking the room at *Escape* in my name had set off some red flag.

My frowned deepened when I realized it was Penelope at my door.

I opened it without hesitation, welcoming the only person I knew whose plight almost identically mirrored my own. The difference was, she was *so* much younger, and honestly... had gotten it worse.

And yet... she was absolutely thriving.

The bright smile on *her* face made me reconsider my own expression—obviously, there was nothing wrong. The realization allowed my shoulders to relax, and I greeted her with a hug she happily returned as she stepped in.

"Shouldn't you be headed to campus?" I asked her, still wondering what could have brought her by.

She answered me with a nod. "I will, but... I kinda wanted to run something by you, if that's cool?"

"Of course. What is it?"

I wasn't expecting what happened next—her tossing her purse onto my couch and turning around, lifting her shirt. Confusion had me frowning again until my eyes settled on the skin of her back—covered in what appeared to be marker doodles.

"Um... Pen, you're going to have to help me out here... what am I looking at?"

"Damn... is my drawing that bad?" she laughed, letting her shirt drop back down as she turned to me. "I was in the mirror with a marker. I know it doesn't look like much of anything, but I'm thinking about getting some tattoos. To cover... you know. The scars."

Just the mention of them took my breath away, and I had to close my eyes for a moment. I'd purposely *not* focused on the ever-present remnants of a horrible run-in with a client she wore on her back.

She wasn't even "*of age*" when she got them, which made the whole thing even sicker. And then, insult to injury, the disfiguring scars had gotten her deemed no longer "pristine" enough for a *Petal*.

They'd sent her away.

I knew Penelope from before the Garden fell, as one of my pupils. Part of my "privilege" in the Garden had been an appointment as an instructor, teaching hair, hygiene, makeup.

It disgusted me now, but back then, there were so few areas to find enjoyment that I'd reveled in my position of helping care for those girls.

Penelope's love for me soothed some of the immense guilt I carried for my role in "training". I was often ridiculed and harassed by other, crueler instructors for building relationships with my "students", but... who the hell else was going to show them any genuine kindness or care?

Who the hell else would've gone after one girl, concerned about her welfare after learning she'd been sold off like cattle?

None of them.

No one else.

Maybe none of them would've wound up captured, and in the very predicament they were trying to save someone from either though, so... there was that.

Alicia had been the one to do all the rescuing.

"So you decided to do it?" I asked, pulling myself from my musings to give my focused attention back to her.

She nodded. "Yeah. I think I want to go to the Heights, to the artist who turned your rose into a phoenix, and did

Tempest's for her. That way I'll know for sure I can trust the work. And get a chance to see Temp."

"I bet she'd love that," I agreed. "And Tristan was an amazing artist. And I think it's a good idea to have it covered— or, camouflage, whatever he can do. It'll help you put it all behind you."

A smile spread over Pen's face. "I really think so too. It feels like… I dunno, like a last step, you know? Tempest said she felt an almost immediate difference once she had her ink, and I'm hoping the same happens for me. I don't want to look at any of it anymore, or deal with people asking questions if my back is out. I want to be free, from all of it. Is that how you felt after?"

"Honestly?" I sighed. "Not exactly. I'm glad to not have to look at it in the mirror anymore, that's for sure. But I didn't have a grand reawakening moment like Temp did, unfortunately. That's not to say *you* won't though."

"I get that," she nodded. "And I definitely want to consider all sides, not get my hopes up, all that. *But…*"

"From a purely aesthetic point of view, it still makes sense."

She grinned. "Exactly. So, on my next break from school, I know where I'll be. You wanna come with? We can spend a few days in Sugar Valley on the way…"

"Girl, nobody is enthralled with those mountains except *you*," I laughed. "Besides, I'm already about to be gone for a few days, so I'll have to see what my schedule looks like."

Pen's eyebrows went up. "Gone for a few days? You haven't said anything about a trip."

Shit.

Her pointing out that I'd outed myself took me so off guard I couldn't even form a quick save. So instead, I shook my head, grabbing her hands as I met her gaze. "You cannot tell *anybody*."

"Oooh, don't do that to me," Pen begged. "You know I'm going to break as soon as Alicia looks at me. Don't tell me any details—plausible deniability," she suggested. "I mean... assuming you're safe..."

"I'm fine," I swore. "And I *will be fine*. And I'm sure it won't take much to track me down anyway. Just... go to class. I don't think anybody is on high enough alert to ask about me within the next few hours, and I'll already be halfway to where I'm going by then."

Pen nodded at first, but then a mischievous squint took over her face. "Dosh... you're not... going to meet a *boy*, are you?"

"What?! Of course not!" I denied, dropping my hold on her hands. "Why would you even think that?!"

Her eyes went wide. "Why are you so scandalized by the thought?" she laughed. "Is this some, *after what we've been through* thing or something? Because I felt like that too at first, but now... these college dudes look *good*. The football players?" she let out a dreamy sigh that made me laugh as I shook my head.

"No, it's not *that*. I think it's great for you, that you're interested in dating and all that-you're an attractive, young woman, it's incredibly normal. I just personally... haven't had anyone that gives me that feeling."

Pen blinked, hard. "*Really*? Not even like... Cree's fine ass?"

I frowned. "Ew. I mean, yes, he's very handsome, but he's basically my brother. He's basically *your* brother," I added.

"Basically is not *actually*," was her response to that. "And his ass looks good—no disrespect to Alicia. Him, Loren's firefighter boo, some of those *Thorns*. Jesus. There's this new one Alicia had a meeting with like a week ago and *sheesh*. Everybody's too old for me though—so, I'm keeping my eyes on the campus guys."

"Which is where they belong," I laughed.

"They aren't too old for *you* though." Pen shot me a smirk. "You're going to tell me you haven't thought about Wilder and those shoulders?"

"Not really—and not *only* because Wilder has a thing with Tamra."

Pen huffed. "Okay, fair point. But, what about the new guy? Have you seen him? He's got this crazy scar that somehow makes him *finer*. It's crazy."

Wait a minute…

"A scar… like, down his face?"

"Oooh, so you *have* seen him," Pen grinned. "He is… *whew.*"

"Yeah, I have." I bit down on my lip, scrubbing my teeth over it a few times before I continued. "You remember me telling you about this Thorn I had the biggest crush on, who got sent away?"

Pen's eyes went super wide. "*Yes.* Oh my God! That's him?!"

"Unfortunately."

"Unfortunately?! How?!" Pen shrieked. "Dosh, he looks so freaking good, and there're no rules now, and—"

"It's not happening."

"Why though?!" she whined, and I laughed.

"Don't you have class?"

"That can wait. What do you have against this dude?"

I shook my head, moving toward the front door in hopes she'd take the hint. "Nothing. I'd just rather not embarrass myself again."

"You don't think he's attracted to you or something?"

"I think he's attracted just fine," I admitted, my face growing a little warmer as I remembered his concern about what would happen between us if he came into my house the other day. "I just don't think we're interested in the same things."

"What does that mean?"

I let out a huff, then moved to open the door. "I tell you what—I'll tell you when I get back, okay?"

Pen rolled her eyes, then grabbed her purse to hike up on her shoulder. "*Fine.* But I won't forget."

"I wouldn't expect you to," I laughed, planting a quick kiss on her cheek as she left.

Once she was gone, I took a deep breath, relieved that the surprise visit had been nothing to worry about, but simultaneously exhausted from it.

Yep.

Definitely time to get on the road.

"WHERE ARE YOU?"

It was probably a bit sadistic of me, but that question, nearly four hours into my drive, made me smile.

I'd removed any tracking I knew about from my cell phone, laptop, and car, and I hadn't even told Pen where I was going. If they'd gone to her already to ask questions, she had nothing to give up.

There *was* the minor matter of my email confirmations for the trip, which I'd downloaded directly to my laptop and then deleted from the mail server.

If she wanted to know bad enough, I guess she could check my banking transactions. But maybe she didn't feel like it was quite that serious yet.

"I'm safe, not being held against my will, nothing like that," I answered Alicia, completely relaxed as I lounged in my seat, my foot pressed evenly against the pedal as my car chewed through the miles.

"Is Isaiah with you?"

"If he is, he's a lot more skilled than I thought, because I'm looking around and definitely alone," I told her. "Which is exactly what I want, if that's okay?"

"You say that as if someone is constantly down your throat here, Dacia."

"Aren't they though?"

I was being a brat, sure.

But *she* was being dismissive, downplaying her overbearing habit of worrying about me. I never felt alone anymore, and coming from a scenario where I had to retreat into my mind just to get some peace, the way she went about her desire to keep me safe was kind of... overwhelming.

"This isn't cool, Dacia."

"You're completely right," I told her. "It's *not* cool for a supposedly grown, supposedly free, supposedly independent woman to not be able to take an impromptu road trip without having to make sure she isn't being followed. It's *not* cool to have babysitters hired for you behind your back. It's *not* cool to have a sister who thinks you're too naïve, or too stupid, or too... whatever the fuck, to take care of yourself. *None* of that is cool at all."

For a long time, the other end of the line was quiet. So quiet, for so long, that if it weren't for the steadily ticking call time displayed on my console, I would have thought she'd hung up.

"At least tell me where you are. Please?"

I rolled my eyes. "Why are you even asking? I'm sure you'll know soon enough. Surely one of your people will have rifled in my trash or something and found out."

"I'll call everybody off. Just tell me where you are, promise to take care of yourself and... call me every day. And I'll call them off."

Shit.

"I'm... still on the road right now," I admitted. "But I'm on the way to *Escape* resort, out in California."

"California?!" Alicia replied, her voice raised until she tempered herself halfway through the word. "You... just up and decided to drive to *California* without telling anybody, and you want me not to worry about you?"

"It's not even a full day of driving, don't be dramatic," I

said. "I just want to be to myself. See something different. And I want to go swimming."

"Swimming?"

"Yes, swimming."

It had been one of my favorite pastimes as a little girl. Later, as a Rose, I'd hated the water - an intense, unexplained aversion. I never quite understood why they wouldn't just train it out of me. Of course, I understood now that the Garden had *given* me that apprehension. One of many perverse therapies from the cruel mind of Etienne Belrose.

I had touched nothing larger than a bathtub since claiming my freedom, but between the lagoon, the ocean, and the pools at the resort, I planned to change that this week.

How *lovely* would it be, to finally see some forward progress, some transformation after being stuck in place for what felt like a year.

"What's going on, Dacia? Are you trying to get my attention? Because I promise you, baby sister, you have it. Do you need to talk to someone? Do you need—"

"Alicia, I'm doing what I need to do, if you could just… hear what I'm saying, instead of charging off with whatever it is you think I'm trying to tell you. You know where I'm heading. I'll be here for a week. I said I'd call every day, and I'll stick to that. Bye for now, I gotta go."

I wanted to finish my drive in peace.

Without giving her a chance to respond, I ended the call. It took all my discipline and commitment to personal responsibility not to turn the phone off too.

That wouldn't be wise.

So instead, I hoped beyond hope that Alicia would give me the space I was so clearly asking for, and not call back.

She didn't.

I was able to finish the drive uneventfully, allowing my

mind to float into my peaceful, fictional worlds. By the time I arrived at *Escape*, I was honestly ready to pull out my laptop. The breezy check-in process and motorized cart to take me right to the front door of my private villa only contributed to that cause.

This was already proving to be an excellent idea.

I ordered myself some room service, took a long bath, and then got comfortable in front of a window that looked out onto the lagoon. It wasn't private in the sense of me having it totally to myself, but the guest list for the resort was small and exclusive.

It wouldn't be exactly teeming with people.

The main building housed the front desk, restaurants, bars, and other amenities, with two floors of guest rooms above everything else. The lagoon was where people like me, who were staying in one of the twelve villas. Everyone else had private, beachfront access to the ocean.

I plan to get some of that too, later.

For now, the sun starting to fade over the lagoon was the perfect backdrop for me to put some words down. And I did, so completely absorbed that by the time I came up for air, the sun was completely gone from the sky, and the only light outside was a combination of torches lighting the edge of the lagoon and moonlight streaming down.

A completely different vibe from earlier, but still beautiful.

I'd eaten more than I should at lunch, so dinner wasn't even on my mind as I closed my laptop, venturing out into the surprisingly cool night. After a few minutes on my private balcony, I decided to trek further. I wanted to see more of the property since I skipped the offered tour when I arrived.

I'd probably just ended up doing it again later, when it was daylight out, but for the moment I wanted to get out and about, and walk around.

Without feeling like somebody was watching me.

Finally.

———

I USED to wish I were a mermaid.

One of very few childhood memories that hadn't been stripped away and replaced with horror. I would hold my breath, eyes wide open, head under the surface as I skillfully cut through the water, playing pretend that I was some great, mythically beautiful creature.

Maybe that's what compelled me back to the water after so much time away - this one good thing I pulled from unfortunate scraps.

The resort was quiet enough that no one seemed to notice or care that I was heading down the dock in the dark.

It was a crisp, beautiful night. The resort guests outside were too absorbed with their own pursuit of peace to pay me any mind. Besides that, I didn't know any of these people, and they didn't know me.

What a freeing thought.

It made it so easy to just put one foot in front of the other as I headed down the pier with a singular focus on my destination.

The water.

I took my sandals off, but nothing else, as if the idea that I was crazy might need any contributing factors. Maybe Alicia and everybody else *should* be worried about me.

I *wasn't* crazy.

But if I was… hell, didn't I have plenty of reason to be?

After surviving what was intended to destroy me down to the core, I was *still here*. Not unscathed, and not without a daily struggle, but… I was here.

Now if I could just progress beyond that.

It was a goal that felt out of reach, but a challenge I was willing to undertake.

Starting with taking a deep breath and confronting this manufactured fear by slipping into the water.

At first, it was so cold that I had to bite my lip to keep from squealing aloud. During the day, under the blazing heat of the sun, the water likely maintained a perfect, balmy temperature. Now though, under the palliative light of the moon, it was much cooler.

Damn near unbearable, but the acclimation happened quickly enough.

I was no stranger to discomfort, so I stayed right where I was, treading water until the liquid lapping against my skin no longer felt in contrast.

I wasn't afraid, or nervous, or anxious.

We were in harmony.

So I closed my eyes, streaking through the water to swim like I hadn't in a long time.

Too long.

My limbs took on a life of their own as I plunged deeper, holding my breath to get under the water, so clear and perfectly blue green with the white sand underneath reflecting the moon I even had a bit of visibility.

Underneath the water, I was deprived of my senses of smell and sound. I had to rely on only what I could see in front of me, only the sensation of the water against my skin, the sand under my feet in the shallow parts. Nothing could touch me out here - nothing could *hurt* me. Not at this depth, not so close to the beach.

And if something *crept* its way from the darker depths, it wouldn't be anything I couldn't handle.

I was in control here.

I was in charge.

I had the power.

It was therapeutic.

No sooner than that thought crossed my mind, something shifted.

There was a discordant sound, too muffled by the water against my eardrums for me to tell exactly what it was—and too far outside my line of sight. An uneasy feeling clung to the pit of my stomach, making it churn as I used the last bit of air I had to see what was coming behind me while I still had camouflage of the water before I had to break the surface.

It was already too late.

My mouth opened in a scream as I was gripped around the waist, instantly, inadvertently welcoming water into my airways —an amateur mistake I should have known better than to make, but the ocean had lulled me into a false sense of security.

I tried to dig in, but the arm secured in a tight grasp wouldn't budge. I was dragged up to the surface, choking, coughing, struggling, still trying to fight to get away.

With no luck.

After what seemed like forever, I was unceremoniously dropped, and I could feel the soft grit of warm sand underneath me. I took a second to collect myself, coughing up the water before I opened my eyes, staring up at the blue-black gradient of the sky, occasionally dotted by the bright luminescence of a star.

It was beautiful.

And even though I definitely had more pressing matters at hand, I let the visual calm me as I caught my breath. Whoever had dragged me from the water had put a bit of distance between us now, which could work to my advantage. As soon as I could, if I could, I was taking off running. It benefited me to appear calm for now.

Resigned.

This survival tactic had been trained into me.

"If you're thinking about running… don't," a male voice sounded from just outside my peripheral.

A familiar one.

I pulled my gaze from the sky to follow sound of the voice, landing on him, partially shrouded in darkness. He was fruitlessly trying to wring the water from his clothes.

"What the hell are you doing here?" I asked, pushing myself up into a seat as I coughed up the last the of the ocean water from my lungs. Of course I knew there was a chance he'd been following me this whole time, but… a girl could dream.

His face, startlingly, frighteningly handsome caught the light as he turned to me looking a bit confused, but still somehow wearing a smirk. "Why else would I be here, Dee? I'm trying to keep you alive."

Eyes narrowed, I pushed up onto my knees in the sand. "What the *hell* does that have to do with you snatching me out of the water like a crazy person?"

"What does keeping you alive have to do with not letting you drown yourself in the ocean?"

"Drown myself? *Drown myself?* Why would you think—"

"Well, you walked into the water with your clothes on, then you went underneath and I didn't see you come back up so…"

"It's called swimming. What does it matter to you what I wear while I do it?" I asked, staggering to my feet. A quick glance around told me we weren't far from the pier I'd walked off of, and the main building of the resort was just a few minutes up the beach.

"Well, most people put on a bathing suit to swim, and they do it during the day, or they use their pool. You have a whole ass villa to yourself, a private lagoon. You can't do your late-night swimming there?"

"*What does it matter to you?*" I asked again, taking a few steps back.

Isaiah gave me this exasperated look and then pulled off his shirt, apparently tired of trying to wring it out while it was still on. The moon illuminated his bare skin and my gaze landed on a perfectly sculpted, thick bicep.

More specifically, the ring of thorns tattooed around it.

Oh.

Yeah.

Of course.

"I'm supposed to be keeping you alive. So with that interest in mind, I would prefer we keep the risks to a minimum."

"So Alicia lied to me?" I asked, finally making that connection. Now that I thought about it, I was furious to see his face here after she'd all but sworn she was going to call the protective detail off. She'd said she would leave me in peace, and yet here I was - *not* being left alone.

"… She didn't lie to you," Zay said, wiping a stream of water from his forehead. "I came on my own."

"What? *Why?*"

"Because I'm… worried about you."

I scoffed, pushing my wet hair back off my face. "Worried about me for what, Isaiah? You don't even know me."

His gaze narrowed at me. "I know enough to know there's something up with you. You gonna look me in the face and tell me I'm wrong?"

No, of course I wouldn't.

Couldn't.

Because overwhelming restlessness had led me here.

Sure, the desire to write was a convenient add-on, but honestly? I was looking for something else too. *Something* missing that I couldn't pinpoint or identify.

It was maddening.

Still though.

"Before a few days ago, I hadn't seen you in a decade, Isaiah. You think you can just read me now?"

"Couldn't I always?"

That question took my breath away.

Because... yes, he could.

Which meant he *had* to know what he'd done to me.

"Just come on," he said, when I didn't reply. "It's getting chilly out here, and I can't have your ass with pneumonia."

It *was* getting chilly, so I wasn't about to argue.

He was the one to retrieve my shoes from the pier, and we caught a few strange looks on the way back to my room. But mostly, people minded their business. It was one thing that had drawn me to *Escape*.

I didn't want to be stared at, recognized, or hell - *talked to,* unless I started the conversation.

I just wanted to... *be.*

Instead of stopping at the beginning of the bridge that led to my villa, Isaiah walked me to the door.

"Go in your room, dry yourself off, and go to bed. You're in for the night," he said, with an air of authority I didn't feel like he had - or *should have* - over me.

"According to who?" I questioned, eliciting a smirk that set off foreign tingles over my skin.

"According to *me*," he said, tipping his head as he leaned in toward me. "Take your ass in the room, so I can go to mine and get the sand out of my crack. Please."

I rolled my eyes. "Well, since you said *please.*"

Without looking back, I keyed my way into the door, closing and locking it firmly behind me. The first thing I did was head for my cell phone, which I'd purposely left in my room because I didn't feel like being bothered.

So much for that.

I turned on the screen to find several texts from people I

loved, all checking in with me—no multiple messages, no missed calls, just… checking.

Which was fine.

I responded to the messages to give them peace of mind, and then I *did* dry myself off, like Isaiah had demanded.

I had no intention of going to bed though.

five

"YOU NEVER DID like to listen, did you?" Isaiah said, taking a seat beside me with a drink in his hand.

I gave him no verbal response.

Just smirked.

Instead of following his demand, I'd set out for the resort's main area—More specifically, the bar.

There were several laid out across the property, and I chose what seemed to be the quiet one — no space for a dance floor or anything like that. Subdued music, couples sitting close at the tables that dotted the main floor space.

I'd chose a corner to myself, tucked away from everyone, and got a soda to sip on while I just… watched.

I'd known it wouldn't take him long to show up.

"Nope. Not particularly," I answered, finally, but not giving him any eye contact—partially because I didn't want to chicken out on the attitude I was giving. Inexplicably, I couldn't seem to shake this undercurrent of annoyance and anger I was feeling toward him—juxtaposed against the undeniable excitement in my chest at having him around.

Which contributed to the *other* reason I was having trouble looking him in the face.

I was a little alarmed by how uncomfortable he made me feel.

Not like I was afraid of him, or thought he would do

something to me. It was something else, something foreign and familiar at the same time.

"So what I'm hearing is, you will not make this easy for me?"

"Make what easy for you?" I asked. This time, I looked up, meeting his gaze.

A mistake.

The dark golden depths of his eyes were intoxicating, and made it even harder to sit still.

"Making up for lost time."

My eyebrows shot up, and I took a gulp of my soda, shifting my attention to… anything else.

"Is that something that feels necessary to you?"

"Very much so, Dee."

I scoffed, tamping down a fresh burst of that excited feeling with a shake of my head. I wasn't about to let myself get too happy about the idea of his interest when the actual history between us was no sweet, tidy story.

"The last time we spoke—before I saw you the other day… you told me I was just a job to you. I was funny, and I was pretty, but you were only there, protecting me, because those were your orders. All the talks we had, the laughs we shared, the… the dreams, and fantasies about if we weren't what we were… if we were something else. Something *free*… you told me you were just humoring me. That none of that had meant anything to you." I stopped, because it was hard not to, when saying those words—*his* words brought that whole thing back to me. When I looked to him, he looked somewhere else, draining the dark liquid from his glass into his mouth. "Did you think I forgot?"

"Did I *think* so? No, not at all. Hoped, maybe."

I shook my head. "Too bad. I remember *all* the bad stuff." I blinked hard, trying to smother my impending tears. "Too much bad stuff, actually. I'm not the same girl anymore. So I'm not sure why you think you can just skip back into my life, and everything will be like it was again."

"I don't want things to be like they were," Isaiah spoke, reaching to grab my hand. My heart jumped to somewhere in my throat as I watched his fingers weave together with mine. "If things were like they were before… we couldn't even do something as simple as this. Me sitting here holding your hand, Dee… can you imagine the world of trouble?"

I pulled away, clasping my hands together so he wouldn't attempt that again. "I can't, actually. Because I can't imagine a Thorn doing such a thing unless it was part of the assignment. *Thorns only have feelings when they're supposed to. Only when it applies to the task.* Remember?"

"Dee…"

"Why did I never see you around the compound before?" I asked him, attempting to shift the subject. "You were really recruited just for me? How? How did she even get in touch with you?"

"Well… like I told you before, I'm a private contractor," he answered, surprisingly playing along. "I loosely crossed paths with your sister earlier this year, so she knew the quality of my work. She had a mutual acquaintance get in touch with me, when she needed me."

"Oh. So you're *not* becoming one of her Power Rangers then?" I inquired, making him laugh.

Another mistake.

The warm rumble of his voice?

Made me want to squirm.

Not to mention, he was pleasing to the eyes as he'd always been. Just… older, and more battle-worn. Those beautiful teeth and full lips, his exquisitely chiseled features artfully marred by the kind of scars you only got from doing risky shit…

I… didn't know I had a "type" until right at that moment.

I'd finally pinned down what that "strange" feeling was.

Attraction.

"Nah, the *protector of the people* thing is not my style at all," he answered, once he was done laughing, and looking at his empty glass. "But... I guess you already know that. I left you, and then... wasn't there to protect you when I should've."

The poignant regret in his eyes when he said that was almost overwhelming, so much so that I looked away before replying.

"It's really not your fault," I told him—and myself, because I'd needed the reminder on more occasions than I cared to remember. "It was kept under wraps, from everybody. How would you have known?"

"I *did* know," he countered, and my eyes flew back to meet his, waiting for an explanation. "I mean... I didn't *know*... like the details of it. But before, I would hear whispers of your name, might catch a random glimpse of you on a Garden security monitor. But then... there was nothing. And I could just *feel* that shit, that something was off. That something was wrong. But I didn't know who to ask, to keep either of us from becoming a target. I asked Tamra to put out some feelers, but you know how it was. There wasn't anybody I could turn to for answers."

I swallowed, hard, trying to process all of his words, but the thing I landed on to reply to was, "So... you knew Tamra?"

"Yeah. We... were as good friends as I guess any of us could've really been."

I couldn't help the dry laugh that leaped from my throat— actually, *laugh* was a much kinder interpretation for the wounded sound I let out. "So... you *had* friends then? And a Rose, at that."

"Dee—"

"It's fine. *Really*," I lied, right to his face. "I don't need you to explain. You did nothing wrong. We were kids, and you had orders, and nothing could've come of it anyway, right? It was probably for the best, that you killed any notion I might have about... whatever it was I had notions about," I finished, too embarrassed by my juvenile fantasizing to even fully verbalize what I'd thought back then. "Imagine if we'd liked *each other*. What a mess."

"I don't have to *imagine*. It's seared in my memories."

Those words made all the moisture disappear from my mouth. So I did what any normal person would do, and swallowed the rest of the contents of my glass, nearly choking on my ice.

"Why are you telling me this?" I asked once I'd cleared my throat.

"Because I want you to know that it was never one-sided. I said what I said because I *had* to. It had to be killed and buried, Dee, because I thought... what if they did something to you, to get at me. To make me colder, to make sure there wasn't anything I cared about, or so I'd know they could take it?" His jaw tightened as he stared across the room, some possible trauma playing in his head. "I was young and didn't know any better way to do it. I just didn't want you to get hurt because of me."

I smiled—a sad, hollow one, but a smile, nonetheless. "If breaking my heart was the goal, you did a magnificent job," I told him, with no malicious intent. "The thing is, though... I still ended up hurt. By you, yes, but... a lot worse, too. Things I can't even think about, shit that only comes to me in nightmares. And you wanna know what's crazy?" I asked, as the tears I'd been fighting finally started making their way down my face. "Even after you made me feel like I was crazy, even after you left... when I was at absolute rock bottom, wondering if I would even see the next day... I prayed for you, Zay. Because you were the only strong person I knew who gave a shit about me—*maybe*. I would squeeze my eyes shut, and pretend I was back at the Garden with you—training, or talking, or… *whatever*. And would pray so hard, that God would send you for me. That I'd open my eyes, and my nightmare would be over, and you would be there to save me. But you never came."

"If I'd—"

"Don't *say that shit again*," I hissed, louder than intended, drawing eyes in our direction. Immediately, I stood, heading out of the bar.

Of course, he followed.

"Dee—"

"I don't—"

"*Stop*," he demanded, not allowing me to speak over him again. He was taller than me, larger than me, and his golden eyes were narrowed, filled with frustration. Isiah was frightening, but I wasn't afraid, not at all.

I was… brokenhearted, *still*, and tormented by my past, and rendered unworthy. I didn't feel like those were things he could even begin to understand.

"Dee… I'm sorry," he said, bringing my fingers to his lips to kiss my knuckles. And… somehow, from that simple gesture, much of the tension in my shoulders, the vexation in my chest melted away. "I'm sorry that I wasn't there when you needed me. And that I broke your heart. And that… I was too much of a coward to come to you sooner. On my own—not because your sister asked me to watch over you."

I frowned. "What?"

"Your face was on the news," he explained, pulling in and pushing out a deep breath. "I saw you there, with Alicia. They were talking about you being Adam Pelletier's daughters. It wasn't even a new picture—it was from when you were kids. But I knew it was you. It was what brought me to Vegas in the first place. But I got there, and just… I couldn't follow through."

When I pulled my hands from his, he didn't resist. "Why not? What did you think was going to happen?"

"I… thought you'd confirm what I heard about what happened to you," he admitted. "Not with your father's murder and being brought to the Garden. The other stuff… Maxim and Sebastian."

I took a step back, trying not to give in to the caving feeling in my chest. "You were okay with coming back to the girl that got away from you, but not if she's been *that* defiled. Right?"

"What? *No,*" he insisted, but I'd already turned to walk away, back to my villa for the night.

Walking, and then, ridiculously, running.

And he let me, for a bit—probably so he wouldn't get security called on him for chasing me down. I was conscious of him still behind me, at a distance, but it wasn't until I was back at the door of my villa, my hands shaking as I tried to unlock the door, that he stopped me.

"Dacia."

Just my name on his lips, and my fingers stopped moving.

I *could've* gotten away from him, could've been on the other side of the door, but I couldn't make myself do it.

He grabbed me by the wrist, tugging until I willingly moved to face in his direction.

"Just leave me alone," I whispered, trying to avoid his gaze. But then he cupped my face in his other hand, lowering his lips to mine, and…

It was almost like the entire world stopped, right then, with Isaiah's body pressed against mine, firm and soothingly warm. His fingertips traced along my jaw, down to my neck, skimming my collarbone before finally resting at my neck, holding me there. At the same time, his other hand moved to the small of my back. Holding me there, too.

Not that I was going anywhere.

I would rather have died than leave the warm embrace of his arms.

He nudged the seam of my lips, and I let them part, inviting the warm rasp of his tongue into my mouth, savoring the oaky-sweet remnants of whatever he'd been drinking earlier. Every move he made, I tried to do the same, hoping I was giving back as good as I was getting.

But truthfully, I hadn't been kissed like this since... *ever*.

I'd never been kissed like this.

And it was everything my teenaged self used to imagine. *More*.

His hand pressed against my back, urging me closer than we could possibly get. Still, I fucking *tried*, pushing my body into his as he devoured my mouth with a level of passion, of intimacy that I...

Didn't even have words for.

And then he pulled away.

Much, much sooner than I wanted him to, which was never, despite my request from just moments ago.

He bit his lip and stepped back, giving me this heated, hungry look that made me squirm.

"I'm... gonna leave you alone, like you asked," he said. "Mostly. I'll be here, while you're here, but I won't bother you. I just wanted to make the point that if I thought you were... whatever it is *you* seem to think you are... would I have kissed you like that?"

I... didn't answer.

And I didn't think I was supposed to.

I found the presence of mind to do precisely what I'd done the day of our last run-in—I got myself behind a locked door.

HE KISSED ME.

.... *Finally.*

On multiple levels, it was information I wasn't even sure how to process - especially when, the next day now, my lips were still tingling with the lingering sensation of his touch.

What the hell was I supposed to do?

How was I supposed to *feel?*

A knock on the door startled me from my thoughts, and my heart immediately started racing with the possibility that it was Isaiah. Shaky legs led me toward the door, where that notion was quickly dispelled.

It was just room service, delivering breakfast.

Breakfast that went uneaten as I... continued processing.

I processed while I showered, while I dressed, while I contacted my friends and family to keep them from descending on this place like a SWAT team if something was wrong. I even processed while I was supposed to be working, spending most of my hours in front of that lagoon-view window with my mind on Isaiah instead of the book I was supposed to be writing.

Now that I wasn't so absorbed with my own feelings, with the anger from the way things ended between us... I wondered what had happened to *him.*

Surely being a Thorn hadn't been sunshine and rainbows.

It was practically an impossibility.

I hadn't been tasked with the others' killer mentality, but I knew how the Garden operated. I knew how they manipulated, brainwashed, and brutalized their clippings into line.

They called it cultivating.

But I knew and loved Roses who'd been through it, and I knew the stories they had. And if *their* experience was traumatizing, I could only imagine what someone larger, stronger, had been asked and expected to do.

The only way it wouldn't have worn on him was if he were a sociopath, and if I knew nothing else about Isaiah, I knew he wasn't *that*.

No matter how hard they tried to make him.

That was probably why he had to go—the proximity to me was keeping him too human, keeping him from the full potential of icy callousness aspired to for most Thorns. As strong as he was, as superhumanly powerful as he'd always felt to me, there was always still this surprising tenderness to him.

Zay made me laugh, taught me hand-to-hand combat, kept me from feeling like there was nobody else in the world who gave a damn about me.

Falling in love with Isaiah had been remarkably easy.

Hell, maybe that was why love stories were standard for me.

Maybe I wanted to see others hold tight to something that had always remained just outside my grasp.

I never got the chance to exchange those words romantically - never knew what it was like to wake up next to someone I adored, never fought and made up, never did the overwhelming majority of things my characters got to do.

Perhaps I'd been living a bit vicariously.

More than *a bit*.

And maybe I'd been doing so for too long, and that's why now, what had been so easy didn't flow as smoothly anymore. I had to come on whole writing retreats now to get it done, and now that I was here... hell, I couldn't even do that.

This was too much.

If I dwelled too long in that place, my brain would take me somewhere I didn't want to go and keep me longer than I wanted to stay. So I closed my laptop and put on a bathing suit to spend the afternoon by the pool.

I was bold as hell about it, putting on a two-piece bathing suit. Then, right before I was getting ready to step out the door... I turned around, grabbing a swim cover up just to feel a little less exposed. Going out to sit by the pool was enough stretching for me today, probably.

Baby steps.

Unlike my previous trips out of the room, I took my cell phone this time, more as a security measure than anything. The oversized shades I was wearing would ensure my ability to people watch and observe, which was much more of an appealing thought to me than immersing myself in the happenings on my cell phone.

I found myself a quiet spot and under a cabana, leaving the drapes open so I wasn't completely closed off.

Another baby step.

Once I was settled in, my gaze swept the entire pool area looking for a familiar face and body. To my mind, there was no question that Zay was lurking around here somewhere to monitor me.

I hated that I found that comforting.

Wherever he was, he was well-camouflaged, because after several sweeps, I still hadn't spotted him. Eventually I gave up, turning my attention to the real reason I had to come out here.

The people.

A few others seemed to be here alone like me, but mostly it was couples and families. It was the families I was most enthralled by, especially seeing how different these people were compared to what you might see as the stereotypical, luxury vacationing family.

They were actually having fun with each other.

It made me wonder what *my* family might have looked like once upon a time, even though the answer was likely nowhere near as warm and fuzzy as the one I might want. Alicia and I had different mothers, and while there was no doubt in my mind that her mother would have been accepting of me, *my* mother was indifferent at best to Alicia at every opportunity.

I hoped Alicia didn't feel too burdened by that.

Paloma wasn't very fond of me either.

The gunshot wound on my arm was proof.

"*Fuck,*" I whispered to myself, trying to clear that train of thought.

I was supposed to be relaxing, not mentally rehashing my traumas.

This could've been an excellent time to sample one of those colorful fruity drinks so many people were carrying around. I could use a bit of alcohol to dull my senses.

But it was specifically for that same reason that I barely indulged, not after my battle with addiction after the whole thing with Sebastian and Maxim.

Fuck.

There I was again.

"Would you like to order some lunch now?"

I looked up to see a smiling server standing nearby, waiting on me to answer. I returned the smile, and *yes*, actually, I *did* want to order some lunch, since skipping breakfast was finally starting to catch up to me now.

Maybe if I had some sustenance in me, it would be easier for my brain to not keep heading back to sensitive things.

It didn't go like that though, not exactly.

What *actually* happened was that I got a pleasant distraction, in the form of a couple, a man and a woman, who came to occupy the vacant cabana next to me. They weren't close enough together that them choosing that one over other empty ones gave me any weird vibes.

I'd chosen that one because it was in the sun, but oriented in a way that it wasn't in my face, and also had a magnificent view past the pool to the ocean. So it made sense that others might choose it for the same reason too.

And besides that… they were cute together.

Very touchy feely with each other, lots of kissing and laughing and teasing, without it being over the top, or seeming like too much.

They were just having fun.

Eventually though, I had to put my eyes back on my own proverbial plate, because I kept getting caught staring by the female half of their duo.

Well… maybe not *caught*, since there was no way she could see my eyes. But I was definitely already looking at them every time her eyes came in my direction, so maybe I was just feeling guilty.

I started preparing my defense when she climbed out of the pool with her gaze locked on me, using a towel to blot the salt water from her natural hair before she padded over.

"Hey," she spoke. "I hope you don't mind the question, but what did you have for lunch? I keep getting whiffs from your plate, and it smells amazing."

"Oh," I responded, relieved that it was that. "I had the jerk wings, yellow rice, and salad with mango dressing. It was a huge portion—too much for me to finish by myself, but it was good."

She smiled. "Nice. I've been trying to decide what I want to get. David is talking about, *we just ate, you're going to make yourself sick*. But I mean… isn't that kind of the point of being on vacation? Doing stuff you're not supposed to do before you go back to some soul-sucking job?" she asked, dropping to a seat at the end of my chaise. "I'm sorry — I'm Melanie," she said, extending a hand in my direction.

"Dacia," I responded, returning the gesture.

"Is today your first day?" She asked. "Or have you been here before?"

"My second day—and no, I've never been here before. You?"

"We just got here this morning, and I have already talked to three other people who say it's not their first visit. And I'm like, I thought the place just opened, and you've already been here before, multiple times? What kinda jobs do they have and are they hiring?"

I laughed. "Yeah, that *is* quite a bit of vacationing. What do you do?" I asked—the making of conversation with strangers was a *Garden*-bred habit I hadn't yet shook. Talking to people was part of the allure, as much of the skill-set as sex.

"Boring ass accountant—is how I'm *supposed* to frame it, but I actually love it. It's just exhausting. David and I actually met at work, at a corporate accounting firm. Fell in love, got married, and now we have our own little boutique firm—that we've managed to *still* make stressful," she chuckled, her gaze caught on her husband as he finally climbed out of the pool too.

I… couldn't blame her.

He was attractive and well-built—so was she, honestly. I found my gaze drifting to his arm though, making sure there was no band of thorns on his bicep. I'd already looked for the rose on Melanie.

Of course, neither bore any markings from the *Garden*. Why would they?

"What do you do?" Melanie asked, touching my leg to get my attention. The contact was brief, but still left me flustered – it was something I was still working on.

"Oh, um… I write romance novels," I answered, watching

her face to gauge her response as soon as the words left my mouth. In Vegas, there was rarely any occasion to answer such a question, since I was primarily surrounded only by those who knew me.

All of whom thought there *was* no job.

I couldn't say *why* I'd given that answer so quickly, but it was out there now, and it made Melanie smile.

"*Really?!* I love romance novels – do you use a pen name? I think I'd remember if I'd seen *Dacia...*"

"I do write under a pen name – that I can't tell you, so I can stay anonymous," I added, hoping she'd just accept that answer.

"Ohhh, mysterious!" she squealed – apparently finding the idea exciting. "Hey babe," she greeted David as he approached us after drying off. "Dacia, this is my husband, David. David, this is Dacia – she writes *romance novels!*"

"Ah, hell," he replied to that, but in a good-natured tone that told me he was just teasing his wife. He offered a hand in my direction, and I accepted his firm grip and shake. "Nice to meet you, Dacia, but I'm gonna tell you now – Mel is about to talk your ear off."

"Man shut up," she said, poking him with a raised foot as he laughed. "Anyway – Dacia. I've gotta know... are you writing the steamy stuff, or nah?"

Honestly?

Just the thought made me blush.

"No, my stuff is super tame," I admitted, shaking my head. *Maybe **too** tame.*

"I try to just keep a tight focus on the actual relationship," I told her, parroting something I'd read in a review and held tight to – *here* was the justification I needed.

"You don't think sex is an important part of the relationship?" Mel asked, wearing a confused frown. "I definitely understand that it's different for different couples, and some people are *asexual*, so their intimacy might look different too, but—oh shit, I'm sorry," she exclaimed, putting a hand over her mouth. "I don't mean to imply something is wrong with the way *you* want to tell your stories."

"No, it's fine," I insisted, waving her off. "You're… actually right. It's something I've had on my mind a lot—part of why I came on this trip, as a writing retreat. Something in my work was feeling a little stagnant, or… like I wasn't giving the stories everything I should. And I think that missing sexual intimacy component might be the thing." I pushed out a sigh, and then muttered, more to myself than anything, "And I have no clue how to fix it."

"Oh honey," Mel soothed, reaching to touch me again, this time leaving her hand planted on my knee. "Are you… kinda… in a dry spell yourself?"

"Melanie!" David scolded. "Could you not…"

"It's just a question!" she defended. "She doesn't have to answer. You don't have to answer," she repeated to me. "I just know sometimes inspiration in *any* area can get hard when there hasn't been any… *release*," she half-whispered, with a little squeeze of her hand. "Everybody goes through dry spells, even married – hell, *especially* – married couples. So it's important to try different things, keep it fresh, have new experiences, you know?"

She'd been easing closer to me as she spoke, to the point that she was almost right beside me now. Instead of having to reach to touch me, our arms were practically brushing against each other.

"Mel… babe, you're doing too much," David said, in this warning sort of tone that still, somehow, seemed rather amused.

"You think so? I don't think so," she said, turning to me with a smile. Her gaze dropped from mine to scan my body, for *just short* of what would've been uncomfortably long. An uneasy feeling started in the pit of my stomach, just before she moved from cupping my knee to grabbing my hand. "*I* think that maybe we could help Dacia with her inspiration problem." She met my confused, questioning gaze with another smile. "David is rather... gifted," she smirked. "And very, *very* generous. I promise, you'd leave here with something to write about."

"Mel..."

"Just – come to our room for some drinks," she suggested, and *that* was the thing that made me pull my hand away. Not that I was exactly comfortable with *any* of this suddenly-confusing exchange, but all I heard now was that they were trying to get me intoxicated in their room.

I no longer felt safe.

"Babe, there you are—I've been looking all over this place for you."

The soothing effect of Isaiah's voice was nearly instantaneous, and the sight of his face?

I could cry with relief.

"You making some new friends?" he asked, *clearly* amused as he looked back and forth between Melanie and David.

David took the opportunity to introduce himself and Melanie, while I just watched.

"So I see *inspiration* isn't the problem," Mel teasingly whispered to me, nudging me with her shoulder. "Whatever that man is planning to do to you, looking like *that*... write that shit down. Instant bestseller," she declared, then stood, looping her arm through her husband's. "Babe, let's order our food, and leave these two lovebirds alone."

Lovebirds?

"Woman, I *know* you're not trying to rush *me* off, like you weren't just trying to scis—"

"Shut up and *walk*," Mel laughed, and they went on, just over to the pool area bar.

Isaiah just watched.

"Hey," I said, popping up from where I'd been sitting to get beside him. "They were trying to get me to go to their room and drink. I don't feel right about it. Like they…"

"Wanted to fuck you?" Isaiah filled in with a grin, presenting a possibility that… had *not* been the first thing on my mind. "Why do you look so surprised?"

I pulled my eyebrows down, shaking my head. "I… I don't… that's just not what I thought. I thought… they wanted to kidnap me."

"Well, yes," Zay agreed. "Just not for nefarious reasons."

"Still. I'll pass."

He smirked. "You sure?"

"Yes, I'm sure," I snapped, returning to my seat, and putting my sunglasses back on.

Now that I knew I wasn't *actually* in danger, I hoped Zay would move on, back to wherever he'd been lurking before. Instead, he joined me on the wide chaise, taking up more than his share of space.

"That *inspiration* thing Mel said to you. What was that about?"

"You heard that?"

He shot me a look, then nodded. "Uh, yeah, half the pool did. Mel is very drunk, and very loud."

My eyebrow went up. "Drunk?"

"Yeah," he laughed. "She's not sloppy, or slurring, but… I can tell by the way David is trying to keep her corralled. He's letting her have her fun, but making sure she's taken care of."

"That's nice," I said, and there must've been something in my tone, because Isaiah gave me a look.

"You know you could do that too, if you wanted? If you want to have a drink—or too many—while you're here… I will not let anything happen to you. Ever again."

Shit.

That was my cue to go.

"I appreciate the offer, but um… I actually think I'm going to head back to my room," I said, getting up again, and gathering my things.

"Am I supposed to come with you?"

I frowned. "Why would you come with me?"

"Aren't I supposed to be doing something to you for you to write a bestseller about?"

My eyes went wide, but I said nothing. I just finished gathering my stuff so I could go before I turned *too* red from embarrassment.

I hadn't, and *wouldn't* start thinking about him like that, in that context.

I wouldn't even let myself form the thought.

seven

*"I NEED **to talk to you. -Penelope"***

That text from Pen at *precisely* that time was just about perfect, because I needed the distraction of talking.

I'd been back in my room from that whole encounter with Melanie and David for hours now, and it was still looping in my head.

I felt like an idiot, and it was keeping me from writing.

Or at least, that was the excuse I was using now.

Truthfully?

I probably wouldn't have been writing anyway, because I would have been obsessing—still— about Isaiah instead.

I gladly closed my laptop and shot Pen a text back, telling her I was free. A moment later the phone lit up with an incoming video call, but when I answered, Pen's face wasn't the only one on the screen.

Alicia was right beside her.

"Is this some kind of setup?" I asked, and they both laughed as Alicia shook her head. "I didn't even want her to call you with this right now. She's just excited and can't hold it in."

"Okay… well, I *definitely* want to know what's up now."

Pen beamed into the screen. "Remember those *fine ass* football players I told you about? One asked me to go to the movies with him," she practically sang, and her excitement made me grin too.

"Okay, and what did you say?"

"I said *yes*, duh! Didn't you hear me say he was fine?"

"I did," I laughed. "But I know that's not the *only* thing, right?"

Pen rolled her eyes. "No, he asked in the library - where he was to get away from the rest of the team and their nonsense, because *he* is serious about his studies. So he's not a bad influence. And did I mention his *shoulders?*"

Beside her, Alicia rolled her eyes.

"Oh my God, Ace, *why* are you trying to kill my vibe?" Pen fussed.

"I'm *not* trying to kill your vibe! I... just feel you might be getting a little too excited, a little too soon. I don't want to see you get your heart broken over this little boy."

"Nobody said anything about my *heart*," Pen giggled. "Sis, I want his mouth on my mouth. I know that's something you're far removed from, *Mrs. Consensual Kissing with My Fine Ass Former Detective*," she teased Ace. "But me and Dacia, we haven't had lips *we want* on us, in... ever. And it's overdue. Please tell her, Dosh."

I... couldn't move my mouth.

And because I couldn't recover fast enough from being put on the spot, my guilt was extra-obvious, Penelope and Alicia both peering into the screen—one set of eyebrows raised, the other set furrowed.

"Okay, so *hoooold* up," Pen said, propping a hand under her chin. "Let me find out you in California *kissing!*"

"You tell Isaiah he'd better hope I don't find his ass," Alicia hissed at the screen, which made my eyebrows go up.

"Wait a minute, *I* didn't say anything about Isaiah — how do you even know he's here?"

Alicia rolled her eyes. "*Of course* I know he's there."

"So he *is* here working for you?"

"No," she sighed. "And he'd better be glad, or I'd have people on his ass right now. I told him to back off, but he said he wanted to stick around and look over you. And… no, I didn't exactly push the issue because *I wanted* somebody looking over you. Which apparently was a mistake since he can't fucking follow directions."

"And what directions, exactly, did you give him?" I asked.

"To keep his hands off you- the same directions I gave before I knew y'all were damn teenage sweethearts," Alicia huffed.

I shook my head. "Why?! *Why* do you think *you* need to regulate that?"

"Because you're…"

"Because I'm *what*? Too stupid? Too weak? Too naive?"

"Just not *ready*," Alicia filled in, dispelling my notions of what I thought she was going to say with an alternative I didn't find much better.

"According to who?" I asked, more upset about it than I probably should be, because it wasn't as if she was wrong, I just…

Why did she feel like that was *her* place to decide?

"I'm just trying to protect you, Deuce," she said, in a soothing tone that only pissed me off more. "I don't think a rogue thorn who broke your heart is who you should use to… I don't even know what you're doing, because you won't talk to me."

"Do you think maybe *this* is exactly why I don't? Because you storm in like Captain Save a Sister when you don't need to. I understand that you're worried about me, and that you feel guilty about what happened. But have you ever considered that it's harder for me to move on because *you* are so stuck in the past?"

"Guys, we're supposed to be talking about *meeeeee*,"

Penelope interrupted, and I knew it wasn't because she was just that self-centered. She was trying to keep this from turning into something it didn't have to be, but I wasn't feeling that charitable.

"If I want to pull out every trick I learned in the Garden and fuck Isaiah's brains out for the rest of the week, I will. Or maybe I won't. Either way, it's not your damn business."

"Can I just say for the record," Pen spoke up before Alicia could, "that my therapist has been clear with me, that it's vital for women who've been through the things we have to reclaim our sexuality, on our own terms, whenever we feel we're ready. Dosh, if that's what you're doing, I think that's a good thing."

"You are not even twenty years old yet, shut up," Alicia told her, pushing her out of the camera frame. "Listen to me, Dosh. Please don't—"

I'd never know what the rest of that please held, because I hung up.

As far as I was concerned, I was done with that line of conversation with Alicia, because if it were up to her I'd be in a convent somewhere probably, never to be touched again.

Wait.

Why does that sound so bad?

Do I *want* to be touched again?

Could that be why all my interactions with Isaiah seemed to fluster me so bad? I'd been around other men in the time after the Garden, with varying levels of comfort. Never before though, had anyone brought out the face-heating, acceptable torture I felt around him.

As if him being the *first* person to make me feel that way correlated somehow to him being... the *only*.

That was ridiculous though...

Right?

Maybe you'd know if you'd taken David and Melanie up on their offer...

Okay.

Now I was *definitely* being ridiculous.

A glance at the time told me that if I left now, I could make it over to one of the restaurants and squeeze in a late dinner. I had the option of ordering room service, but I needed to make myself more comfortable being out among people, experiencing things.

It helped that both my dinner and dessert ended up being excellent.

As much as I enjoyed the meal though, I couldn't help continually looking around, checking over my shoulder. The obvious thing was looking for Zay, but the more insidious possibility was someone with less-than-good intentions watching, stalking me.

And I didn't want David and Melanie sneaking up on me either.

It was with that vigilance in mind that I made my way back to my room after dinner, trying to not be completely obvious about it, while taking care to mind my surroundings. Part of me was focused on that, the other part still mulling over... everything. My brain was teeming with information, but the one subject that kept beating them all had me stopping at the door to my room, taking a seat on the bench outside instead of going inside.

It didn't take very long for Isaiah to get the message.

I zoned out for what seemed like just a moment and then there he was, sauntering across the bridge.

"Is this your way of letting me know you need to speak to me?" he asked, and I sat up a little taller, swallowing the pesky nervous butterflies he'd set off.

"It's not as if you've offered me another option."

He stopped in front of me, giving me that ridiculous, sexy smile. "Would you have taken my number, if I tried to give it to you?"

"Probably not," I admitted.

"Right." He took a few more steps forward, enough to sit down beside me. "Good thing I put it in when you weren't looking."

"What?"

Instead of offering any sort of apology, he shrugged. "So you'd know who it was, if I called."

"You say that as if it's some normal thing."

"It's incredibly normal, Dee. Depending on how you look at it."

"*Not* as a trained assassin is how I'm looking at it."

He shrugged. "Maybe you should reconsider."

"Maybe *you* should."

That made him pin me with a look that wasn't exactly a glare, but was no less intense. "Why does it feel like you're trying to pick a fight with me?" he asked. "Why don't you just tell me what it is – what reaction, whatever – you're looking for, and we can skip the extra?"

"I'm not looking for anything from you," I defended, not sure those words were true even as they left my lips. "I just figured we could... talk?"

A smirk spread over his lips as he sat back, stretching his arms across the bench to get comfortable. "Okay. What is it you want to know?"

"I want to know... what happened to you?" I said, meeting his gaze. "Like... after they separated us. Where did you go? What did you see? What did they make you do? How did you get... this," I murmured, boldly reaching forward to touch his face.

He tensed, but didn't stop me, letting me just barely skim the pads of my fingers over the raised abrasion.

"You sure you want to know?"

"I wouldn't have asked if I didn't."

He grabbed my wrist, very suddenly, but not roughly,

moving my hand from his face. "This is because I asked too many questions about what would happen to you when I was gone," he admitted, and well… now I knew why he'd asked if I was sure I wanted to know. "As you know… we weren't supposed to have any real attachments. Sex was fine, homies were fine… but anything more than that, especially before you'd really been outside the Garden, was a no. So… I paid for it."

"I'm *so* sorry."

"Don't apologize," he said, squeezing my hand, which made me realize he was still holding it. "It's not your fault. Not your shame, Dee. To answer your other questions though… I've been everywhere. Seen a lot. Done some unspeakable shit." He shrugged. "And now… I've been trying to find some normalcy with this "private contractor" shit, but honestly… I don't even know what the fuck that is anymore. I don't know what *I* am anymore."

My eyes lifted, surprised in a way that he'd divulged something like that to me. But in other ways… maybe it wasn't remarkable at all.

This had been our dynamic anyway, before the forced rift between us.

"*Normal* for a Thorn… that's not what you want to do anymore, is it?" I asked. "Surely that's not who you want to be?"

He shrugged. "It's what I know how to be."

"That's doesn't mean that's how it has to be though," I countered. "You never *wanted* this… none of us did, not really. So… just do something different. That's within your power."

"Is that what you've done?"

I scoffed. "Me? Nah," I shook my head. "I can't say I've managed that yet, but… I'm trying."

"Why just *trying*?"

"I don't know," I admitted. "I'm not sure." I blew out a

sigh, and pulled my hand from his, cupping it in my own to calm the tingles. "I guess I said it as if it were some simple thing, that I've mastered. I just… I remembered you telling me that, in a perfect world, you'd want to play basketball. Do you remember that?"

A grin spread over his face as he nodded. "I do. We had to keep up with the American teams, watch the games, all that. We had to know the trivia."

"And you *loved* it. So…?"

"Dee… I'm too old to be a basketball player now," he laughed.

"I know *that*," I giggled. "I'm just saying… maybe you could be like, a kids' coach or something. Be a mentor. Hell, play some pickup games at the park. I bet you haven't even done *that*, have you?"

His silence spoke volumes. And just when I was about to be smug about it, he sat forward, pinning me with another weighty gaze. "I guess I don't have to ask if you've been swimming, huh?"

I closed my eyes.

I forgot he knew about that—about that fear I'd held of water.

"Is that why you thought I was drowning myself?" I asked, shaking my head. "You thought I'd use my fear to destroy me?"

"It's exactly the kind of poignant thing I'd expect from you."

I smiled, pointing my gaze up at the sky, where about a million stars had burst, breaking up the midnight-blue canvas.

"Come on. Let's go inside."

I didn't wait on a response from him—I just went, knowing he would follow. Really, I had no clue what I was doing, or why my brain had gone there, but I headed straight across the villa for the patio doors that would let us out to the other side.

I had spent no time out here yet, but it was beautiful. Big

planters lined either side of the deck, creating privacy from the other bungalows and forcing the view out to the lagoon. During the day, the pergola and white fabric shades offered coolness and protection from the sun.

Now though, the moon reflecting off the lagoon made them an ethereal blue-green, and it was… romantic.

Why the hell did I bring him out here?

I turned around, intending to redirect our path back inside, but Zay had already stepped out onto the deck with me.

Blocking the door.

"Have you tried it out yet?" he asked, gesturing to something over my shoulder.

"Huh?"

"The pool."

I turned around, and my gaze fell on the tiny private pool he was referring to – one of the selling points of getting one of the larger villas, actually, but…

"No," I answered. "I haven't."

He raised an eyebrow. "Not as over the fear as you thought?"

"I am."

"Okay then… let's swim."

Before I could even react to that, he was already taking his clothes off.

I couldn't do anything but watch.

I expected him to stop at his boxers or something, but no— he stripped to nothing, and then climbed his beautiful, naked ass into my pool like he belonged.

And then grinned at me.

"Come on in, Dee. The water's nice."

I swallowed.

Hard.

"I'm gonna grab a bathing suit," I said, knowing exactly how ridiculous it sounded.

With his arms propped up on the side of the pool, Zay shrugged. "Whatever makes you feel most comfortable."

Shit.

When he put it that way, it made me wonder if getting a bathing suit, instead of just stripping, was… *childish*. Which, the opportunity to revel in, and outgrow that quality had been taken from me, so if it *was* childish, maybe I was within my rights.

But… the longer I stood there, wrestling internally with the choice, the less comfortable I became with the idea of… leaning on comfort.

And before I could talk myself out of it… I stripped too.

While *he* watched.

I got my ass in that water for a *little* camouflage as fast as I could, but still… it was a step, right?

Now if I could just go to the other side of the pool now, where Isaiah was waiting for me.

Maybe.

Waiting to do… *what?*

There wasn't time to think about it really, because he took it upon himself to come to me when I didn't go to him. Before I could put up any kind of resistance, his arms were around me, holding me close in the balmy water.

"What are we doing right now?" I asked, forcing myself to meet his eyes. "What is the purpose of this?"

"You invited me inside," he countered. "We can do whatever you want."

"What if I don't know what I want?"

"What if you do?" He shrugged. "What if you know *exactly* what you want, but… it's wrong of you? But you want it anyway?"

"Who says it's wrong?"

He smirked, and his hands dropped, skimming my skin under the water. "Your sister, for one," he said, fingers pressing into my hips as he pulled me against him. Even under water, I could feel how hard he was, and in that moment, I was confident that if this were any other man, that would've repulsed me.

Because it was Isaiah, I maneuvered a hand between us, to grab him, and squeeze. "She's not here right now though, is she?"

"*Fuck*," he whispered, and then his fingers were in my hair, holding me in place as his mouth crashed into mine. Like the first kiss, the world stopped, but this time, there was nothing reserved about the way he devoured me, like I was some long-lost treasure of his.

Like I… *belonged* to him.

And shit… maybe I did.

It was the only semi-logical explanation for how easily I simply melted into him, not just comfortable in this sudden ramping up between us, but *comforted* by it. With one of his hands gripping my ass, his other fingers grasping the back of my neck, his dick hard against my stomach, and his tongue in my mouth, I felt more grounded, much more *alive* than I had since… I wasn't sure when.

Maybe never.

It didn't matter.

What mattered was that I wasn't some ruined doll who'd been used and abused too much to be valued. I hadn't realized how badly I needed that assurance, that *certainty*, until right in this moment, and… maybe this wasn't even about that.

Maybe it was just sex.

But… maybe I needed *that* too.

It certainly felt very, *very* urgent, as heat built between my legs, and a coil of pressure tightened in my core. It was effortless to say yes when Zay asked if I wanted to go inside. I enjoyed it immensely when he physically *carried* me there, and then spread me, wet, across my bed and just stared at me like he was seeing me for the first time.

In a way though… he *was.*

We'd been absent—physically, at least—in each other's lives for nearly a decade. We'd seen too much, experienced too much, to be the same people now.

And yet… this was still very much the boy I'd fallen so inappropriately in love with—and maybe it was still inappropriate now.

I didn't care.

And if he did, he didn't show it, his golden eyes darkened with lust as he climbed onto the bed with me, and spread my legs apart.

He settled between them but didn't enter me, like I expected.

Instead, he kissed me—my lips, my forehead, my jaw, my collar—soft, slow, lingering things that made me squirm underneath him.

When I complained, he went slower.

Down to my breasts, where he nibbled and licked, caressed and plucked with his fingers.

Begging made him go *even slower*, which pissed me off, but I did what he was demanding—laid back, so I could just enjoy it.

And… *God*, there was so much to relish—the feeling of his stubble on my skin, the firm caress of his hands, the soft insistence of his lips, the warm rasp of his tongue.

I held my breath as he traveled down my stomach, squeezed my eyes tight as he bypassed my center to cater to the insides of my thighs, fisted the sheets as he finally, generously, brought the perfection of his mouth to my clit.

He lavished my pussy with attention and praise, with his fingers, his mouth, his *nose.* Mentally, I wasn't sure I was equipped for the kind of gratification Isaiah seemed so intent on heaping between my legs, but I was willing to pass out from the effort.

He pushed his fingers into me in deep, searching strokes that made my stomach clench as I whimpered in pleasure. Between his fingers and his mouth, I was right on the edge of bliss and he was pushing me higher with every stroke, every lap of his tongue, every indulgent sound from *his* lips, like I was the best thing he'd ever tasted.

It was too much.

And not enough.

And then I was over that cliff, yelling my throat raw as an unfamiliar current of decadent pleasure ripped through me. For a moment, there was no sound, no sights, no nothing, just… *goodness.*

I'd barely caught my breath before Zay was on top of me again, with his face smelling like… *me.* I had no complaints as he brought his mouth to mine, pushing his tongue between my lips to kiss me as he settled between my legs.

"You liked that, huh?"

Instantly, I stiffened.

An icy feeling skittered over me, settling in my chest as I shook my head, trying to clear away a sudden rush of unpleasant memories.

"Don't…," I closed my eyes, then quickly decided it was better to have them open. "Don't say that to me, okay? Please? It's—"

"You don't have to explain," Zay interrupted, the concern in his eyes making me feel like shit, even though I *knew* it should be the exact opposite. "We can stop."

"I don't *want* to stop!" was my vehement response, but I could tell from the look on Isaiah's face, he wasn't about to give me a choice. "I… *please.* I just… I can't stop… *here,*" I explained, knowing it wasn't enough, but still hoping he would understand what I couldn't find the words to properly verbalize.

When I felt his fingers on my clit, I knew he had.

He knew I couldn't leave the moment we'd just had—before my bullshit—on *that* note.

And it was seemingly nothing for him to take me right back to that feeling, with his hand between my legs and his mouth on my neck.

On my breasts.

On my pussy again.

I was in that same place again, my body feasting on his attention when he brought his mouth to mine again.

Made me cum, again.

Relief sank through me as I collapsed back onto the bed, already spent. That lightened feeling was interrupted by confusion as Isaiah settled beside me, instead of... *inside* me.

"I think we should call it a night there," he spoke up, before I could, as if he could already see the question in my eyes. "Don't you have a zip-lining thing tomorrow?"

I frowned. "I'm not even going to ask how you know *that*. I'm going to focus on telling you—I'm *fine*. We don't have to—"

"*Dee*," he spoke up, in a firm enough voice that I stopped talking. Instead of saying anything else, he just extended his arms, and I... settled against his chest, instead of arguing.

Likely saving us *both* the embarrassment of me trying to change his mind about us going any further tonight.

Especially since... I had no idea how I was going to react to that anyway.

That hadn't really been one of my considerations, but maybe it should've, since so much of what was supposed to be an enjoyable act had been connected to trauma for me.

Just because I liked Isaiah, just because I *wanted* him... I shouldn't have assumed that would make it all just... breezy.

So.. I should probably just take the win.

And a *win* was exactly what it felt like, being nestled against him, surrounded by his arms. I had no clue what this meant for us, no clue what was next, but… I refused to think about it either.

Cumming twice was exhausting enough.

eight

WHEN I WOKE UP, Zay was still in my bed.

Not exactly unexpected, but certainly not... _expected._

Especially not him being fast asleep – seemingly devoid of the usual hypervigilant awareness I'd long associated with Thorns.

As I watched the steady rise and fall of his chest, I convinced myself that it must be some sort of trap – he only _looked_ utterly at peace, not on high-alert against possible impending danger.

I pulled the covers off him to test the theory.

He stirred, and shifted positions, then went right back to the same state as before – heavy deep breathing, lips slighted parted, eyelids closed, but relaxed. There he was, in all his utterly nude glory, just...

In my bed.

Like he belonged there.

The idea made me smile—but more than that; it made me act on the slow, steady throbbing between my legs. Of course I understood why he'd stopped where he did yesterday, after my... _moment._

Now that we'd passed that, I wanted nothing more than to finish what I'd started—to reclaim what had been so traumatic for me.

I refused to let the fear hold me back any longer.

So I climbed on top of him.

With my legs straddling his, I took his dick in my hands, marveling over how immediately he came to life at my touch. I could feel the shift in Zay's breathing, the sudden tension in his body. Before he could awake enough to make me hesitate or second-think it, I lined my body up with his and sank onto him.

Luckily, I'd been wet since I woke up.

His eyes came open, and went straight to where we were joined in a perfectly, uncomfortably tight fit. I wanted to move, wanted to ride him, but his hands were locked onto my thighs, keeping me still.

"What are you doing?" he asked, his gaze finally coming up to meet mine.

"What does it seem like?"

"Like you caught me slipping."

I smirked, propping my hands against his chest before I leaned in a bit. "You know... you're right. I should *not* have been able to sneak my way onto a Thorn's dick, should I? You losing your edge?"

He released his hold on my thighs to prop his hands behind his head instead. "More like... settling in."

"Settling into...?"

"Normalcy," he answered, with a little roll of his hips that made me gasp. "It's a foreign feeling, but... I keep hearing it's what I'm supposed to do. So... here I am, I guess?"

"But this is such a vulnerable position," I said, moving my hands up to his neck. I slid a finger along the base of this throat as I tipped my head. "There was this move you taught me... remember? I could kill you."

Not even the slightest tinge of fear showed in Isaiah's gaze as he shrugged. "You could. But I trust you to take this moment and do something else with it. The power here, right now... it's yours, princess. You're in control."

You're in control.

Yes.

I was.

I moved my hands back to his chest for necessary leverage, and then finally took him for a ride. This was yet another thing I hadn't known I was waiting on, not until I was fully immersed in the feeling of him stretching me open, filling me up. His hands gripping my ass and gripping my thighs, his upward strokes to meet my downward ones with full force.

The delicious pleasure of it all.

And then, afterwards... peace.

I didn't feel the least bit compelled to balk at having his arm around me, holding me against his chest despite our need to clean up. It was just... quiet.

But of course, quiet always brought along such pesky thoughts.

"Why do you think they let us keep our names?"

From the way he flinched, the immediate change in his breathing pattern, I realized he must've fallen back asleep.

"What?" he asked groggily, probably thinking he'd missed some sort of lead-in for my out-of-the-blue – to him – question.

I adjusted my position, pointing my gaze to meet his. "You said you heard my name on the news, right? *Dacia Pelletier.* Well, Dacia isn't the most common name. It's recognizable. So you would think, if the idea was for us to become other people, to so easily slip into whatever role the client demanded... you'd think of all the things they took – everything they made us forget... why would they leave us with our names?"

"I've actually read something about that before," he answered, settling in comfortably again, with his thumb tracing a circle on my bare hip. "Supposedly, it's tough to convince someone of a new name – like, it's imprinted on us. You can make them doubt a memory, reshape those memories, alter their entire backstory in their mind. But your *name* is too permanently etched."

I frowned. "What about people with like… true amnesia? Brain injuries and such."

"That's a different thing – usually with stuff like that, there's other damage, to parts you want to keep intact."

"I think you're bullshitting me."

"I'm *not*," he laughed. "Now, I'm not saying it's true, just that I read it, and it made sense. Stripping us of our names without fucking up our brains beyond repair was too much hassle. So we got to keep that, and nothing else. Because they knew they were gonna fuck us up so bad it wouldn't ever matter, not for most of us."

"Why do you say that? That it doesn't matter?"

He shrugged. "Because… even now, I may know my first name, but what else? I don't have a surname, a year I was born, a country of origin, none of that. I'm just… here. And what am I gonna do – get a fucking blood test or something?"

"Why not?"

Isaiah's face pulled into a scowl. "Why, after engaging in international espionage, murder, kidnapping, and whatever the fuck else would I not want to have a blood test?"

"Well, when you put it like that…"

"Right," he chuckled. "So… yeah. Limbo is just my state of being, for now. Unless something big comes back to me, which… I doubt. Have you gotten anything back? Like, from your childhood?"

I shook my head. "Not really. Mostly just… fragments. Alicia thinks it's a slow detox kinda situation. The longer you're out, the more that comes back. It hasn't been very long for you, so… just know that it's coming. And hope that you don't get back anything that should've stayed lost."

"Did that happen to you?"

I pushed out a sigh. "Not a lot, but… some. The night my father was killed and my sister and I were taken… could've gone without that," I told him. "I kinda stopped doing too much prying, after that. Because really, what good can come of it, you know? I've got enough to heal from. And rather spend the time making fresh memories, and just… living."

"But you don't want to leave *everything* back there, right? The time we had together… was that not a wonderful memory for you?"

"Of course it was," I assured him, shifting positions so I was looking at him head-on. "All of that is still clear as a bell. The butterflies you gave me, the excitement of knowing I would see you, the things you taught me about protecting myself… and the fact that you tried to convince me I was just imagining something between us."

"*Shit,*" he muttered under his breath, as his hand moved to rest against the small of my back. "I… guess you've got a point there. But you already know, that—"

"Wasn't what it seemed, yeah," I told him. "But… that doesn't erase the feeling."

"I know. So… tell me how I make it right."

I thought about it for a moment, then leaned in to press my lips to his. "Show me how you *really* feel."

———

HE WAS ASLEEP.

Again.

Since I'd already woken him once to satisfy my urges, I let him be.

Especially since *I'd* woken up in a daze, wondering what the hell I'd gotten myself into, because it definitely wasn't as simple as sex.

I was too calm.

Too happy.

Too… okay.

It was terrifying.

I pulled myself out of bed, grabbing my cell phone as I went so I could place a phone call to the one person I could count on to understand this particular plight.

Tempest.

Like me, she was only *recently* removed from the Rose lifestyle. And even though she and I, like me and Alicia, had been bred with different purposes… she got me.

Tempest was still figuring herself out.

She'd been further along than I had so far, though. She'd started an entire business, and I don't think she'd said the words yet, but if you asked me, she was in love.

A state which had left her on more than one occasion feeling quite conflicted.

So… yeah.

She'd get me.

I hesitated outside on the patio, looking at the time.

It was still pretty early.

But with me in California and her in the Heights, there was a three-hour time difference which would put my call at what was actually a reasonable hour.

So I stopped hesitating, and went ahead and made the call.

Tempest answered quickly, sounding out of breath, which she promptly explained by letting me know she was out for a run.

"It's time for me to cool off though, so I can talk," she assured me as I took a seat at the end of one lounge, wrapping myself a little tighter in the robe I'd thrown on. "What's going on?"

"I slept with Isaiah last night," I blurted, before I could give myself any passes by thinking of a way to make it sound nice and neat. "And this morning. Twice. He's in my bed right now."

"Whoa! *Whoa.* Wow," Tempest exclaimed. "This is how you're coming first thing in the morning?"

"I'm sorry," I told her. "I know it's a lot. I just… I don't know what to do now. Or what to say. Or where we stand. Or how to feel."

"Well, I'm fairly sure the question of *where you stand* is best answered by a discussion with *him*. But as far as how you're supposed to feel… you just feel however you feel. Period. Whatever you feel, is fine. The key thing is to figure out how to deal with it from there."

"Okay, I can tell you've been on time for *your* therapy sessions," I teased. "I hear you," I told her, "I'm just still so… I don't know. Confused."

"Confused for what? Dacia, isn't this man like your long lost first love or something? You told me that, right?"

"Yes, I did, I'm just… The history was complicated enough between us. Just *that* part was enough to deal with and honestly was something I didn't even know how to handle. Now we've added this element of sex to it - and not *just* sex, the first shred of any intimacy I've had with anyone… Pretty much *ever*. And now I just feel way too comfortable. Like I'm *uncomfortable* with how comfortable I feel with this whole thing. Like I should… be more traumatized or something. With everything else, *every other part* of feeling human again has been so difficult. And yet this thing that *should* be major… this just feels like it has come so easily that its kind of frightening."

"Wait, let me get this straight - you reconnect with the first boy you fell in love with, and he is full-blown, grass-fed, sex on a platter. He is still as dreamy and crush-worthy, and all that as you remember. You *finally* get the dick… dick that you *want*… And you feel like it came too easily? Dacia if *anybody* deserves for something to come easily to them… It's you. I'm sorry - I'm *not* trying to be dismissive, I just… really don't want to hear that you feel like something should have been *harder* for you. After what *you* went through. You've got to be kidding me,"

Tempest fussed, sounding more like a trusted bestie than the tough-girl killer I *knew* she was.

Had been.

Not anymore.

I sighed. "I'm pretty sure it's *because* of what I've been through that I feel like this," I explained. "It's like... everything else was so bad, and then *now* everything is... too good. It's like I'm waiting on something to go wrong, because something *has* to go wrong, right?"

"No, actually," Tempest said. "Absolutely nothing *has* to go wrong. Things could just, *this time*, go your way..."

I hoped she was right.

I really *wanted* her to be right, because I hated this feeling, as if I were missing something significant by not freaking out.

Like tragedy was just waiting in my blind spot while I got too comfortable with peace.

Ah.

Peace.

I felt it right in my grasp, so solid, in a way that I probably shouldn't.

But here I was.

And it wasn't even that I was under some teenage delusion that Isaiah and I were going to be together forever now.

I wasn't thinking that at all.

I understood, fully, that not only was Isaiah human, he was a Thorn. We weren't far enough removed from the Garden that those tendencies were stripped entirely from his nature.

He could disappear into the night, never to be seen or heard from again.

He *probably* would.

It wasn't that I thought something like that wouldn't hurt, it was just that... I recognized the possibility – the *likelihood*. But I also knew that if it *did* happen like that... I would be okay.

The recognition of all that didn't make me any more

prepared to, after I've gotten off the phone with Tempest and come back inside, find the bed empty.

And not just the bed, *the room.*

The entire villa.

I swallowed hard, running through scenarios in my mind for what could have happened, before ultimately admitting to myself the most likely truth.

Exactly what I'd told myself to expect.

He'd left.

Remember, Dacia. You just had this talk with yourself.

Yes, I had, but that didn't make it sting any less - especially when a glance at my phone revealed that I'd missed text message from him.

According to the timestamp, it had to have come while I was still on the phone with Temp.

Two words that hurt a lot more than I wanted them to.

"I'm sorry."

Of course he was.

I took myself to the shower where I stayed longer than necessary.

When I finally came out, the first thing I did was strip the sheets off my bed, since I planned on getting right back in it. I was probably spending the day there. The last thing I needed was to spend that time immersed in his lingering scent.

I replaced them with fresh linens from the closet and then dropped the used ones in the bin for the laundry service to pick up later.

My phone started chiming with the standard texts and all of that from Alicia, Loren, Pen, and the others I'd gotten to know all checking in.

I went through the motions of it all.

Really, though… I felt like I'd been punched in the gut.

I *should have expected this…*

But I had not.

A firm knock at the front door of the villa startled me, and I blinked a few times, trying to remember if in my earlier daze I'd ordered room service.

I wrapped myself in fresh robe and went to the door, pulling it open without thinking.

And there on the other side of the threshold was Isaiah.

Holding a bag that smelled like breakfast.

"I… *Oh*," I laughed, breaking into a peal of giggles that made him frown.

"Are… you okay?" he asked, stepping in when I moved back out of the doorway to allow him inside.

I shook my head. "No. Nothing's wrong, I just…when I came back in earlier, and I saw that you were gone, my head just went to…some pretty dark places," I laughed. "But here you are, so…no, nothing's wrong."

I… expected him to laugh at that too.

At least crack a smile over how dramatic I was being.

Instead, his expression remained somber, so much that it made me frown.

"Wait…" I said, propping my hands on my hips. "If you were just going to get breakfast… why did you send me a text saying you were sorry?"

Instead of responding, Isaiah pushed out a sigh and started walking, so I followed him to the kitchen where he put the bag down on the counter. When he finally turned to face me, there was something in his eyes I couldn't place.

"Because I didn't just go to get breakfast," he admitted. "The *I'm sorry* was because I woke up freaking the fuck out about how… *comfortable* and shit I'd gotten. Too far, too fast… too deep. I woke up feeling some shit that… worried me, and I don't like being worried. So I thought it best to find some distance. But I realized pretty quickly, that I couldn't do that to you. And… I couldn't do it to *me* either."

"So… you're telling me that after spending the night in my

bed, and then waking up to each other, and talking, and reconnecting, and all that... you...ran?" I asked, even though I clearly already knew the answer.

Isaiah pushed out another sigh. "I'm not proud of it at all, but yeah. I ran. And instead of it being relieving, I just felt like shit. It felt like a loss, and... I've taken enough losses. So... I got breakfast."

I was supposed to be mad about this.

Right?

Disgusted by his wavering, by his *fear*.

He'd put himself back in my life, brought all these buried feelings back up, and his ass wanted to *run*?

Fuck him.

Right?

If someone wanted me, there should only be absolute certainty, no room for questions in their mind about us.

He didn't get to waver, or waffle... right?

Except for the fact that he was feeling some of the same things I had.

All the same things, maybe.

And instead of *actually* running away from it... he'd come back.

Him overcoming the urge was almost more reassuring than him never having it.

I didn't need some ridiculous blind devotion, didn't need him to not be human. We'd both been trained to suppress whatever *we* needed, to present a specific picture to those who saw us. Our discomfort, anxieties, triggers... our *happiness* didn't matter. And our feelings never took precedence over the agenda.

So, not only were we fighting against what had been ingrained as a natural urge within us, we were up against all the stuff everybody else went through too.

So no, I didn't need any extra, any of the stuff that was

purely about my ego.

I just needed *him* honestly, needed him to keep finding the strength to overcome the urge to not rely on default behaviors. He wasn't a Thorn anymore, and I wasn't a Rose, we were just Dacia and Isaiah. Just Dee, just Zay.

And we were fortunate enough to have found our way back to each other.

So really... Fuck that breakfast.

It took nothing for Zay to pick up on my energy shift and meet me with the same. With my arms flung around his neck, I pressed up into him, and his hands went immediately under my robe, gripping and squeezing my ass as his mouth crashed down onto mine. From there, it was all about finding the physical connection again - robe open, up on the counter, with Isaiah's sweats pulled down around his hips.

It was crazy... as much as I'd imagined myself having a hard time with this, as reticent as I'd been to the idea of a man *touching* me, let alone being inside me... I couldn't think of anything I wanted more than I wanted *this*.

Him.

And maybe that was it - the fact that this wasn't just *any* man.

I don't know that I would have ever been willing to push myself to this zone for a stranger, but with Isaiah... it just felt like the way it should have always been.

Him buried deep inside me, his tongue in my mouth, big hands gripping my thighs while he slow stroked me into a state of bliss.

Maybe it wasn't the vacation I needed at all.

Maybe it was just this.

———

I MADE him come ziplining with me after that.

It was already on my agenda for the day, but was something that I'd considered canceling since I knew Zay would follow me for my protection.

Now that we'd connected, though, it felt a little wrong to put him through such a stressful day while he was in his bodyguard capacity.

So... I decided he would come along as my companion instead.

He didn't complain.

He gave me a long ass look, but he didn't complain.

He went back to his room for a bit after we had that breakfast, so he could get fresh clothes and all that. But he came right back, just like he said he would, and then he and I headed out together.

Even *that* was exhilarating.

Like I'd told Tempest, I still didn't want to overthink this thing between us, but it was tough not to.

Not when he made me feel the way he did.

And so... I once again came back to a feeling of, with everything I'd gone through, if this worked in my favor, I deserved it.

If it didn't... I'd survived worse.

"Hey what's wrong?" I asked Zay, when we were at the tower we'd be diving from, already all strapped into our gear. He had a scowl on his face, and I wasn't sure if it was because I had insisted on doing this despite his – unspoken - reservations, or if he saw something he didn't like and was scoping out the scene.

"Huh?" he said, and I noticed how he kept a firm eye on the expanse of trees we'd be zipping over.

"Hey... you're not... scared of heights, are you?"

"What? Nah, I'm not scared of heights. I'm fundamentally opposed to unnecessary risks."

"*Oh my God,*" I left. "You are *scared of this* aren't you?!"

"I'm not *scared*, I'm healthily concerned about this shit," he corrected as the zipline attendant walked up to us.

"All right, y'all," he said. "Whose going first?"

"He is," I chimed, before Zay could answer.

"The hell I am," he denied.

"You *have* to go first, so you can wait for me," I giggled. "It'll give you the chance to figure out any danger that might lay ahead."

"I'm looking at the danger—it's right there," he said, pointing out at the treetops.

"*Wow*… You are more nervous about this than I am!"

"Considering that your ass seems completely unconcerned, that's not saying that much."

"I'm not completely unconcerned," I denied. "I'm just… very committed to doing this. I've been mentally preparing, and I'm just going to get it done. And you are going to go first and wait for me, right? And make sure it's safe?"

Isaiah blew out a sigh, but he still nodded his head.

And a few minutes later, he fulfilled that commitment by taking off.

Yelling at the top of his lungs, but still.

As the attendant prepped me, I closed my eyes and took a deep breath.

I hadn't told Isaiah that I was feeling in need of a jump start - something to wake me up and remind me I was alive. And that I wasn't committed to whatever narrative Alicia or anyone else had placed around me with the label of *victim*.

Of course, that was *before* I'd woken up with Isaiah in my bed.

With that said, the need didn't feel any less urgent, so I listened carefully to the attendant's repeated instructions.

And then I was off, my body beating against the wind as I sliced through the air, rocketing too fast to catch any of the details. It was just a blur of beautiful trees and sky, a rush of sensation and visual stimulation, and then in what felt like way too little time... my gaze connected with Isaiah's face. I watched him grin at me as I landed safely on the ending platform.

My heart was pounding too fast for me to say much as I was unstrapped from all the gear, but once it was off, I threw myself around Isaiah. He welcomed me there readily, squeezing me tight as unexpected tears of joy, relief, exhilaration, and... I don't know what else came pouring out of me.

I couldn't imagine having done this alone.

The rush of emotion was overwhelming.

Zay didn't question it, he just let me let it all go, with the good sense to remove me from the public eye while I sobbed. It wasn't until we were in the car, going back to the resort, that I calmed myself down enough for him to talk to me.

"You feel better?" he asked.

Yes, actually, I did.

And I told him as much, making sure he understood that it wasn't just about me having done some bucket list zip lining.

It was *all of it*, taken together, that somehow, finally, had me feeling like I wasn't just existing in my body.

I was *here*.

Grounded.

Broken flesh and spilled blood, but I was *here*.

"Did covering the tat help?" he asked, seemingly out of the blue.

But I knew he'd probably been wanting to ask for a while.

"No," I told him, honestly. "Not like it did for some others. Not like I hoped it would."

"But you feel better... with everything?"

"Yeah," I nodded, reaching across the car to where he had both hands gripped tight on the steering wheel. At the feeling of my touch, he relaxed, and immediately moved to entwine his fingers with mine.

No, having the tag covered was no great equalizer, not in the way I'd hoped.

But having him here, being connected to him again?

Well.

That was a different story entirely.

nine

"WHY DO I even need to know this stuff? Isn't this what I have you for?"

I was being a brat, and I knew it, for the sole purpose of having Isaiah send his signature sexy scowl in my direction.

He didn't disappoint.

His thick eyebrows furrowed together, his top lip curling a bit as he fixed his gaze in my direction.

"We've been over this, Dee. Yes, you need to know how to defend yourself. I won't always be around."

Inwardly, I was bursting with butterflies over the nickname - he was the only person who called me that.

Dee.

The way it rolled off his lips, so easily, in that rasp of his... it was literally everything my teenage dreams were made of. But the joy in that quickly wore off as my brain fully processed his words.

"What do you mean you won't always be around? Thorns are basically invincible, and protecting me is literally your job, right?"

"For now," he answered, suddenly unable to meet my gaze.

Nervous nausea pricked at my gut, making a sour taste creep up the back of my throat.

"Are you being transferred or something?" I asked him.

"Nothing for you to worry about," he said, very abruptly locking eyes with me, in a way that made my heart race. "I'm here right now, and we're going to get this down, aren't we?" he asked, in a tone that invited no *dissent. "I want you to be safe at all times, not just when I'm there to protect you. But as long as I'm around… I'll never let anything happen to you."*

―――

"I KNOW you're not in here looking this good by yourself…"

Those words brought an instant flush of heat to my face, even though I was in on the little game Isaiah had apparently decided he wanted to play.

"Are *you* trying to be the person I'm here with?" I asked, shooting him a smirk as the bartender slid me the drink I'd waffled back and forth so long over ordering or not.

A very unassuming vodka and soda that was the entire reason we were even out in the first place.

Well… maybe not *the* reason, but certainly one.

It was our last night here.

Our last night with just us, and just paradise, before we had to make our way back to the responsibilities that came with our day to day lives.

My ability to pretend to be a girl with no other cares than basking in the unfaltering attention of her childhood crush was ending.

Honestly… I was tempted to book a few more days.

But that would just be putting off the inevitable.

"I want to see you in that."

I'd been packing my suitcase back up while Isaiah watched and had pulled down the barely there dress I'd brought along as… a fantasy, I guess. The chances I was actually going somewhere where such an outfit would be appropriate had been non-existent, but it was one of those *a girl can dream* kinda things.

At least, until Zay announced his desire to see it become a reality.

"You mean… right now?" I'd asked, holding the slinky blue fabric against my body. "Why, so you can take it off?"

He grinned. "Yes, but before that… we can have drinks, and dance, and you can enjoy being the sexiest woman in the club…"

My eyes went wide. "*Club?* You think I'm going to a club?"

"Is that… outlandish somehow?"

I draped the dress across my open suitcase and propped hands on my hips. "Uh… yeah, a bit," I told him. "I don't… *do* clubs. Or dancing. Or *drinking*. Or… sexy."

"Well, that last part is a lie from the pits of hell," Zay shrugged, not moving from his relaxed position on my bed, hands propped behind his head. "The other stuff though… you've got something against those things?"

I swallowed. "Um… not necessarily, I guess. I just haven't done them. Not since… everything."

What I wasn't saying, and hoped he'd pick up without me having to, was that those things terrified me. The unwanted attention, the social interaction, the *variables*, losing control or risk of having something done to me, or the possibility of triggering forced addictions… it was all so much.

Too much.

"You know I wouldn't let anything happen to you, right?"

I sighed.

With that one line, Isaiah pulled me from an impending spiral of negative thoughts, keeping me from getting lost in *that* headspace.

"I do," I agreed.

He sat up. "Okay. So… it's one thing if you just don't want to do it because you don't want to do it. We can get room service and chill, that's fine. But if you don't want to do it because you're *afraid* to do it… tell me what I can do to ease those fears."

And now… here we were.

Here *I* was.

In that perfect, slutty dress, in a dark, smoky club on the *Escape* property.

The venue's contained nature helped, but it was Isaiah's presence, warm and imposing, right at my side, that was doing most of the heavy lifting.

He'd left my bungalow just long enough to do his own—light—packing and get ready for our little outing himself. He'd come back looking like a freaking *Sugar&Spice* model and smelling good enough to make me feel like a cat in heat.

He must've liked what he saw too, because we'd barely made it out the door without ruining all our efforts to get dressed up. It was only because he insisted we needed to get over this particular hurdle that I didn't call for a last-minute change of plans.

So *here we were.*

"How do you feel?" he leaned into me to ask in my ear. "You having a good time?"

I peeked up at him with a smile. "I am. I like the music – like the way the bass feels. And I like the smoke, somehow," I laughed. "And… the energy, of all the people. It's electric, and I love it. This though…," I said, nodding at my mostly-untouched cocktail, "I still think I'll pass on. I don't want anything altering my brain while I'm out like this."

Zay nodded. "That's definitely understandable – I'm glad you were willing to test it out, see how you feel and make your decision from there. On your own."

"On my own? What does that mean?"

He shrugged a bit. "I just… I've seen how your sister is about you, you know? And it's not necessarily a bad thing, but… I just wonder how much of your reticence about life in general is less about how *you* feel, and more to do with how *she* feels. She's worried about you so much, and done so much to assure your safety that you've felt you owe it to her."

"Wow. I… don't know if I've thought about it like that before," I admitted. "But honestly, maybe I *do* owe my safety to her. Wouldn't you feel like it was a slap in the face if I were out here doing risky shit after you gambled your life to rescue me?"

Zay nodded. "Sure. If you decided to pick up a life of crime, or… gator wrestling, or MMA fighting or some shit, I'd definitely feel a bit slighted. But… you had to sneak away to go on a writing retreat, Dee," he teased, even though his words were valid. "She had me trailing you to go for a run. You were afraid to just… go to a club," he added, bringing home his point. "I get it, with a past like ours, we have different considerations than the everyday person. And it's smart to mitigate the potential harm. But we can't be so paranoid that we don't even enjoy the freedom we waited so long for. That's a whole other type of bondage, and… we're off that."

"That all sounds really good, and of course I agree. I don't *want* to be afraid of my own shadow. But Alicia is… that's a whole other level of *brick wall* to try to talk to," I explained, but Zay shook his head.

"I'm not concerned about that. Alicia is your sister, not your master. I'll talk to her."

My eyes went *big*. "You'll talk to her about *what?*"

"Loosening the reins," he said, like it was all so simple. "And I know what you're probably thinking, *Alicia is gonna kick your ass, fool.* And… shit, she might, that's a tough ass chick," he laughed. "But… the thing is, our interests are aligned – hers and mine. We both want nothing but the best for you."

I raised an eyebrow. "So… what is this, instead of just having *her* on my back, you want her to scoot over so you can smother me with safety and protection "for my own best interest" too?"

"Not at all," he denied. "Dee, I'm not interested in smothering you. I just… over the last few days of us, together… I've gotten a glimpse of something I never thought would be in my grasp. I didn't know if I'd see you again, didn't know if I'd get to talk to you, touch you... but we're here. And it's been like stepping right into those fantasies we had, all those years ago, of what freedom would be. And I still want more. I want to know the girl I fell in love with when the concept itself was foreign to me, without any inhibitions." He sat back a little, eyes locked with mine, just staring. "Maybe that's selfish of me. I just don't want anything holding you back from whoever you're going to grow into, so I can experience it all."

My lips parted, but it took me several moments to find any words. And even then, I turned away from him with a whispered "*wow*," mortified by what *had* to be a visible blush on my face.

"Did I say something wrong?" Zay asked, and I immediately shook my head.

"No. *no*," I repeated, meeting his gaze. "That was... the most romantic thing I've ever heard, actually," I admitted. "And I... write romance novels for a living, so I don't think I'm easily impressed with such things."

Isaiah laughed, scrubbing an—embarrassed—hand over his head. "I hate to disappoint, but I wasn't trying to be romantic. Just... honest."

"That's what made it so romantic," I smiled.

The corners of his mouth curved down as he thought about for a moment, then nodded. "Okay. Well... I guess in that case... dance with me?"

"Dance?" I actually full-blown laughed at *that*. "It's hilarious to me that you think I know how to dance."

He smirked. "Nah, don't give me that, Dee." He leaned in, placing his hand at the small of my back—which was bare, thanks to my sexy dress. It took everything not to just melt into his touch right there. "You've definitely been bobbing your head, swaying, shaking your ass to the music right here on this bar stool all night. So I know you can keep the beat at least."

As usual, his words to me were not up for debate.

He'd already slipped off his bar stool and grabbed my hand, tugging me along with him. Obviously I went along with it, not putting up a fight, because really… I *wanted* to do it. Although I was not a true *dancer*, the idea of being hugged up close with Isaiah, moving to the bass-throbbing, sensual music that was playing now was beyond appealing to me.

And the act fully lived up to the expectation.

I couldn't keep the smile off my face as we grooved to the music. We weren't doing anything complicated at all, but I still had the good ass time for what ended up being the next *five* songs, ranging from twerk music to slow dancing, not thinking about anything that could go wrong. Just letting all that apprehension, all those worries go, and having fun with my… *date.*

And as it turned out, nothing *went* wrong.

We danced, we went back to the bar for cold—non-alcoholic—drinks and then went back to the dance floor, staying until we were sweaty and tired. And then back to my room, where we made love right on the floor by the entryway.

Afterwards, we showered together and then ordered super late room service. Then fell asleep after we overate.

The next morning, I woke Zay up for one last round on those luxurious sheets before we had to get on the road.

Not at all the trip I'd set out to take when I booked it, but… freaking perfect.

Instead of driving, Zay had hopped a flight to California to come look after me. That decision ended up working in our favor. Not only did I have him to keep me company on the trip back to Vegas, but he also insisted on doing the driving, which meant I could recline back and relax while we talked and laughed and just… *vibed.*

Even this part was amazing.

Back in Vegas, I didn't linger too long once we stopped at his place to drop him off, before heading back to my own. He had some things he had to do, which was understandable, since he'd ended up on an impromptu trip to California with me for several days. He had business to take care of.

And really so did I.

Admin work to do, emails to answer, manuscripts to edit, overbearing sisters to check in with. A niece, who had stories and kisses on a backlog, just waiting for me to get back. I knew Alicia was dying to ask all kinds of questions about me and Zay, but she didn't. We just had dinner, and kept it breezy, and… again, *vibed.*

Now that I was recharged from my trip, I was able to enjoy it all for what it was, instead of resenting the loss of self-isolation like I'd found before I finally pulled the trigger on my getaway.

I'd known I needed the break.

Known I needed something different, something new to revive my spirit and pull me back to center.

So… mission accomplished?

"DO you think we may be having *too much* sex?"

From his position alongside me at the bathroom sink, his mouth still full of toothpaste, Isaiah met my gaze in the mirror, eyes wide. He opened his mouth to speak, then thought better of it, clearing and rinsing his mouth before glancing up at me again.

"Is that some type of hint for me to pack up my overnight bag and go or something? You're sick of me?"

I laughed, and then turned to leave the bathroom, since I'd only been hanging around because he was in there--a testament to exactly how wrong he was.

"The opposite, actually. I'm getting a little concerned about the level at which I *cannot* get enough of you. It's a bit alarming."

That was no exaggeration.

In the week since we'd come back from *Escape*, Isaiah had been over here every day.

Not that every single moment of it had been spent having sex, but certainly plenty of it had. I kept waiting for it to start to get old to me, because it *had to*… right?

That fatigue never came, though.

And it had me concerned, to where I'd actually brought it up to my therapist, wondering if it was a sign of something wrong.

"Or, perhaps, something very, *very* right," she'd teased. "As long as you're not neglecting responsibility, or engaging any risky behaviors, I'm not worried at all about you wanting as much intimacy from your partner as they're able to give. You've spent the bulk of your life not even knowing this was possible. *Of course* you're wanting me to absorb it all now. Please don't take offense to this analogy, but… a dry sponge can hold a lot of water."

I wasn't offended.

But she'd inadvertently giving me a new thing to worry about.

Sure, sponges held a lot of water, but only *so much* before you had a mess on your hands.

I didn't want to be a mess.

And *risky behavior*?

Such as putting my heart on the line for a not-so-former killer?

How was that not dicey?

It was quite easy to see the logic of it when I stepped outside myself to focus on the *facts*, not the feelings. But then, pesky reality stepped in and Isaiah's brawny arms around my body, pulling me securely against his chest, didn't feel dangerous at all.

It felt like the safest thing in the world.

He met my gaze. His expression was incredibly thoughtful for a long moment before he finally pushed out some words with amusing difficulty. "The feeling is mutual."

I grinned up at him, sliding my hands up over his bare chest. "That was like pulling teeth for you, wasn't it?"

He smirked. "That's how you know it's real, right?" he asked, not bothering to deny what I already knew.

He was having withdrawal symptoms.

Well… for lack of a better way to express it.

It wasn't as if he gone cold turkey from his *Thorn* activities -

- even up until recently, just months ago, he'd been taking mercenary jobs. So he wasn't as far removed from his *Garden* hard-wiring as some of the rest of us. This time we'd spent holed up, making love and cooking dinner together, talking until we fell asleep... all that was contraindicated to everything we were programmed to be.

"It's been a rough two weeks, but I've got it," he said, planting a lingering kiss against my forehead before he pulled back.

I frowned. "Two weeks? You mean since we ran into each other on the street?"

"Two weeks since the resort..." he answered, giving me a look as if I were the one confused. "I'm saying—it was easier at Escape, when we were insulated—isolated- from everything else. Now that we're back, and I can have you back in my life... I've got to make some sharp adjustments pretty quick. Including some kind of job that doesn't involve... well... You know."

"Zay, it's only been a week since we left the resort."

"It's definitely been two," he laughed. "Check your calendar."

"I don't have to check my calendar, today is what it is, and we checked out of the resort on— oh damn. That was two weeks ago, wasn't it? Why does it feel like..."?

"I guess time flies when you're having fun."

"Yeah," I chuckled, running through a mental checklist trying to make sure I hadn't missed anything while I was confused on what freaking day it was. "Anyway, though," I said, shaking my head free of that as Isaiah pulled on a fresh pair of boxers from his overnight bag. "The struggles are pretty common for us, based on what I've heard from everyone else I've talked to. You... should go to therapy. It really helps. It's helped all of us who've done it."

Isaiah frowned. "And what exactly do you think I can tell a

therapist that won't have me locked in a dungeon somewhere with my ass beat by American cops?"

"We have a network that we trust," I assured him. "There's ways around it. I get it --it's a difficult thing to think about, opening up to some stranger, but... it's not even just about helping. I think it's likely *vital* for us, if we want to be acclimated to this real world, have healthy relationships... *not* see a trauma highlight reel every time we close our eyes. You *need* to talk to someone."

Isaiah's eyebrows went up. "...Why do I get the feeling you're trying to tell me I *have* to do this, if you and I are going to be a thing?"

"I'm not saying you *have* to... yet," I amended, not wanting to downplay the gravity of how I felt about this.

But truthfully, as much as I wanted Isaiah... nothing could come in front of my healing from what I'd gone through. This relationship with him couldn't trump my mental health.

And two people who'd gone through what we had?

I couldn't imagine it not going toxic if only *one* of us was whole.

Isaiah gave me this deep, searching look for long enough to make it uncomfortable, but I wasn't about to back down. Finally, he gave me a brief nod.

"I'll think about it," he said, turning his attention back to his bag before he spoke again. "You know you're the only person who could get away with this shit, right?" he asked, and I grinned.

"Perks of being the love of your life, right?" I teased.

"Oh, is that what you are?"

"*Obviously*. Can you deny it?"

He smirked, shaking his head. "I cannot, and would not try."

"Okay, then there we go. What are you about to get into?"

I asked, noticing he'd pulled out athletic gear instead of regular clothes.

"Well," he said, "You want me to go to therapy, right? Wilder invited me to come shoot hoops with him, Cree, some other guys. I wasn't going to go do that kumbaya shit, but now that we've talked... I guess I'm going."

I bit down on my lip to keep from laughing. "As much as I think it will be good for you to feel a connection and build relationships with some other guys, you know *that* won't count as professional therapy, right?"

Zay sucked his teeth. "*Duh,* Dee. You said some of them have done it already, so I'm going so I can get the lay of the land — not as a replacement. Have a little faith in me."

"Okay, I'm just trying to be clear. And I don't want this to... I just want to be..."

"I get it- you don't have to explain yourself. I know you're not wrong, which is why I'm not giving this as much pushback as I could. Difficult things don't scare me. And once I've decided I want something, it's going to be mine. I want you more than anything in the world, so... if I've gotta do the inner work, and love myself, and all that shit to get you... I guess that's what we're going to be doing."

I couldn't even properly swoon over that moment like I wanted because my attention was drawn by a sudden pounding on the door – urgent, demanding pounding. I frowned, and started for it, but Isaiah immediately grabbed my arm, putting me behind him.

"You stay here. I'll go see," he said, with a look that very clearly communicated he expected me to stay right in that spot.

Of course I *didn't* though, waiting a few seconds for him to make his way through my place to the front door before I was right behind him.

And thank goodness I was.

He peeked at the view on the camera panel and saw that it

was Alicia at the same time I did. Before I could intercept, he'd already opened the door.

Which meant we'd have to talk about Isaiah being over here.

Again.

"Isaiah," she spoke, wearing a forced smile. "Why am I not surprised to find you here? And… mostly naked." From there, she turned her attention to where I was standing, in just a robe. "I see why you stood me up for our workout and breakfast this morning."

"Oh, shit!" I cupped a hand over my mouth. "Ace, I—"

"It's fine. You're… preoccupied."

Here we go.

"I'm… gonna finish getting dressed, and I'll go out through the garage," Isaiah spoke up, clearly trying to get out of the blast radius of this thing between me and my sister. "Good to see you as always, Alicia. And *you*… I'll see you later." He hooked an arm around my waist, pulling me into him again to place a parting kiss against my lips before he disappeared into the back of the house.

Not a nice, *we're in front of people* kiss either.

"Well," Alicia smirked. "You two are just cozy little peas in a pod, aren't you?"

I rolled my eyes. "Which is such a problem for you, for some reason that has me baffled."

"It's confusing for you, that I might have an attitude about you breaking our plans because you're hugged up with some guy?"

"He's not *some guy*."

Alicia huffed. "Right, I forgot—he's the *thorn* who broke your heart a decade ago and gets to just waltz back into your life like everything is fine. I get it."

"He didn't *waltz back like everything was fine*," I snapped. "And let's not forget—*you* put him in my face in the first place."

"Because I was trying to protect you, like I've always done —like I've always *tried* to do. In case you forgot."

"How could I?!" I half-laughed. "You remind me at every opportunity that all you see is some weak baby bird that fell from the nest and broke its wings. You cannot *stand* that maybe I'm ready to try flying on my own."

"*All I want* is for you to fly on your own! I'm just trying to keep you on the lookout for fucking hawks who'll eat you alive!" Alicia retorted, shaking her head. "Or did you forget flying doesn't keep you safe from predators?"

"Again—*how could I?*" I pushed out a dry laugh. "You know… that insinuation, after what *I* endured—beatings, rape, being injected with God knows what, forced to *do* God knows what… that's really wack."

Alicia let out a deep sigh, then nodded. "You're right. And I'm sorry. I know you're well aware of the depths of depravity in this world, probably even more than I am. I shouldn't have said that. I… I am just *worried* about you, Dacia."

"For *what?* I am… just as vanilla as I wanna be," I laughed, for real this time. "I don't *do* anything for you to be worried about."

She raised her eyebrows at me. "The half-naked thorn opening your door this morning says different."

"Right – it all comes back to you not liking Zay."

"I don't *not like* him," she denied. "I just think it's too soon, and that he's a distraction from your healing and shit that you don't need."

"What I need is not up to you," I countered. "And I don't even understand how you can be so against me being in a relationship like you're not damn near married with a kid yourself."

"I'm a lot further removed from the Garden than you. For years, and *years* after I left, I wasn't thinking about being hugged up with someone, falling in love."

I scoffed. "Okay, well, excuse me for not being some machine, where I could just turn my feelings and desires on and off at will, like you apparently could. And maybe still can – what are you set to now? *Ignore my sister's obvious cries for a little breathing room and completely alienate her?*"

Those words brought a sudden flash of anger to Alicia's face, then... *hurt*, before she could temper it back to something more neutral.

"Well... this isn't the first time I've been accused of being a robot, so maybe you're onto something," she said, turning to head for the door. "For the record... I'm not trying to... alienate you, or ignore what you're saying you need, I just—"

"Intention versus impact, remember?"

Her lips pressed together in a line, because of *course* she remembered that concept, drilled into us in the *Garden* as a universal part of our training. No matter what kind of asset you were being molded into, *impact* was always more important than your *intentions*. It was paramount that your actions fell in line with your mission, *intentions* be damned.

"You're right," she finally nodded, after a moment. "I'm obviously not hitting the right note with you. I've *never* been able to hit the right note with you."

"Maybe if you stopped trying."

"How else am I going to make it up to you?"

I frowned. "Make *what* up to me?"

"*Everything!*" Alicia insisted. "I didn't do what I should've back then, so I'm trying to do it *now*."

"Back then?! Alicia, we were *children!* What the fuck were you supposed to have done?!"

"Anything!" Her eyes were wet, and so were mine. "But I didn't, and now here we are."

"It wasn't your job to protect me," I whispered. "Not then. And not now."

She shook her head. "If that's the case... then after the

Garden, after everything... why did you hold it against me? At first, I thought it was just a thing about people from your past, but you were fine with Pen. You're fine with all the others from the Garden. You're fine with Isaiah, who *broke your fucking heart*. But me? You... couldn't even look at me. Couldn't be in the room with me without it being obvious I made your skin crawl, couldn't talk to me. For months, and months, and *months*. But him—you're the happiest I've ever seen you."

"Is *that* what this is about?" I asked, moving to the door where she was standing. "Alicia... they *programmed* that reaction into me, so I wouldn't remember you. They made it so that just the thought of you, was... traumatizing. So I would block it out. I can't take back those reactions I had to you at first, as much as I wish I could. And I'm *so sorry* I hurt you. But it wasn't... it had nothing to do with who you really are and was no indication of how I actually feel about you. I *love* you, Ace to my Deuce," I told her, reaching out to cup her face in my hands as tears spilled down both our cheeks. "And the fact that I'm able to *be fine* with the other roses, the other thorns... with *Isaiah*... is directly because of you. All of this is *because of you*, and I'm so grateful that you loved me enough to burn the world down over me. But... you've got me now, and I'm not going anywhere. So let me breathe. Let me learn. Let me *fall*. You'll know if I need you to pick me up."

Alicia stared at me for a moment before wrapping her arms around my neck, tight. I could barely breathe, but I let it happen without a word, especially once I realized she was sobbing, however quiet.

Of course, I broke down in sobs too.

"Okay, I've gotta go," she said, after several long minutes had passed. She pulled away, quickly wiping her face dry and squaring her shoulders, her resolute expression absolutely ridiculous with red, puffy eyes. "You and Isaiah... come to dinner tonight. Yaya likes him, and she asked about you yesterday."

I smiled, wiping my own face. "We'll be there."

After that, she was gone, now that we'd exhausted our emotional bank for the day. I headed back to my room, expecting to find it empty, but Zay was still there, perched in my side chair with his headphones on.

When I walked in, he looked up from his laptop and then set it aside, pulling his headphones down. "Hoops isn't for another hour or so, so I figured I'd hang out in case you needed me after Ace left..."

He extended his arms to me, and I didn't hesitate to put myself between them, climbing into his lap, head against his chest.

Because he was absolutely right.

eleven

"IF YOU SEE THIS. Sis. Listen. I don't know what—who!!!!—got into you before this one, but maaaaaam! This is IT right here. I had to prop up a fan to read this. Keep THIS up."

"I'm so disappointed. I turned to this author for warm, feel good romance without the vulgarity that so many seem to turn to. And yet, her in this new release, it seems like a completely different author. I wanted to read porn, I'd read porn. Please go back to the content that made me fall in love with your work!"

"Ugh. Again with the short, incomplete work. So they're "together" now. What about a wedding, babies, anniversaries?! I'm so sick of this trend of supposedly "real" romance – I'm here for the fairytale. Only giving two stars cause the sex was hot. Outside of that, you need to go back to the drawing board and tell a whole story next time, cause this ain't it."

"I don't usually leave reviews, but all these trying to tell the author what she should and shouldn't do are pissing me off. DO YOU! I love all the facets of your work, the depth and variety of characters, the different steam levels, all that! It seemed like you really let loose in this one, no restraints, and ended up with a beautiful, steamy story. Everybody doesn't want babies and a wedding-myself included – but that doesn't mean there's any less desire for intimacy and romance. THANK YOU for exploring that, and representing so many different outlooks in your work, without a bunch of unnecessary fluff. Again, DO YOU. You've got a fan in me!"

I sat back with a sigh, absorbing all the different reviews

that had come about from my latest work. I only gave myself a few days to even peek at them, since I didn't want to get too deeply immersed in opinions about my work. Those few days always gave me a lot, though.

I knew I might get some extreme reactions to this latest project, since it included a level of passion and steam the people who read me hadn't seen before – not in *my* work. I was prepared for it though, and as expected, the reviews ran the gamut from *love this, more of it,* to *you're going straight to hell for this, whore.*

Of all the things I might go to hell for, I was quite sure writing sex between consenting adults wasn't one.

When I first started, there was a high likelihood the negative reviews would have really bothered me. Now? It rolled right off my back.

All it took was a reminder that everything was *not* for everybody, and that nothing in an anonymous review had the power to define me, or my work.

Not to mention, no matter *what* was said… I'd heard and endured much, much worse.

Nice try though, internet troll.

I switched away from the page of reviews, to look at the tab where I was doing a bit of loose outlining for my next project. Already, this one felt quite a bit different from my usual too.

I'd always leaned toward the warm and fuzzy, syrupy sweet, but this project felt more like… my natural vibe.

A little darker.

A bit grittier.

Not so polished.

Certainly, some people were gonna hate *this* too.

They would be okay though, and so would I.

My doorbell ringing drew my attention away from my screen, and I hopped up to see who it was. A quick glance said it was Alicia, dressed in nice jeans, boots, and an oversized sweater – a departure from her usual athletic gear that made me check the time and realize I'd lost track.

"*Shit,*" I muttered to myself, opening the door to let her in.

She raised an eyebrow at my robe as she stepped through the doorway. "Going for an ultra-casual look today, or…?"

"Nope, sorry!" I told her, already turning to head to my room. "Just got occupied with work, and lost track. Give me like fifteen minutes, I'm already showered and all that, just gotta get dressed."

"Make it ten, so we can beat her home."

The *her* in question was Penelope – today was her chosen birthday, a tradition that had been her own idea. We'd actually not been able to find much history for all our searching, so she had no idea when her *actual* birthday was.

So she picked one.

Alicia and I, along with some of the others who knew and loved Pen, had spent the last few weeks preparing and planning a surprise party for her. She was officially dating the football player now, and we'd recruited his help in getting her to her apartment at a specific time – a time we were butting dangerously close to.

"Yeah," I yelled down the hall, already yanking my jeans on. "Ten is fine!"

Luckily, I'd already chosen my clothes and fixed my hair before I'd sat down in front of the computer to burn through some time. I was in the bathroom doing a rather haphazard mascara application when I heard— "Hey, what is this?! Is this… a book outline?!"

The mascara wand dropped from my hand, just barely missing my creamy-white sweater as I rushed from the bathroom to see Alicia bent over, peering at my screen.

"This sounds amazing," she said, oblivious to my panicked state. "You should really write this."

I swallowed, hard. "Yeah. I definitely plan to. Next release."

She froze, then her gaze flicked in my direction. "... next? As in... there's a previous one?"

"Several previous ones. This one will be the sixth."

Alicia straightened up. "You've written *six* books?!"

"Five," I corrected. "Number six isn't written yet."

She waved me off. "Fine. Five. Why the hell don't I know about this?! Where are they? Show me!"

I blew out a sigh. "I... don't have any of them here," I admitted. "So I wouldn't out myself."

"*Out yourself*?! As in... you're in hiding or something?!"

"I use a pen name," I explained. "And we really don't have time for this conversation."

"We'll make time," Alicia insisted, propping her hands on her hips. "What's the pen name? What do you write? *Why* wouldn't you tell me this?!"

I shook my head. "Because if I told anybody... I felt like it wouldn't be *just* mine anymore, but you're nosy and were all in my screen, so I guess the secret is out now."

She scoffed. "I'm not *nosy*."

I crossed my arms.

"Okay. Fine. I am. Now, what about what you write? I want to see it. I want to *read* it! It's not about me, is it? Like a whole thing about how much you hate your overbearing big sister?"

"What?! *No*," I laughed. "I... write romance novels," I said, half-expecting her to rib me about it, but her eyes just went wide.

"So I've been getting the life teased out of me by Kingston Whitfield for *reading* romance novels, while you've been flying under the radar writing them? Wow, I've been out in the cold for no reason. Thanks, little sister."

"I haven't even been around him like that to see you get

teased, first of all. Well… no, actually, *first of all* would be… you read romance novels?"

She sucked her teeth. "*Yes*. Why is that always the reaction?" she laughed. "Can a bitch contain multitudes in peace?"

"Sorry. I just… you're so… *tough*."

She sighed. "Ah. Yes. And because I'm *tough*, I'm supposed to just be that one thing, never anything else?"

"No. Of course not," I assured, even though her raised eyebrows told me my actions were giving something else. When writing, I tried my best to fully realize my characters, never boxing them into their archetypal characteristics, because *people* weren't like that.

I didn't want my characters to be… characters.

I wanted them to be real.

So… I should probably be giving my sister the same room.

"I'm sorry," I told her, raising my hands to signal peace. "We're still getting to know each other, right?"

She smiled. "Right. I started reading romance novels because I was trying to understand the phenomenon of love, and how it fits into relationships, all that. I mean… I'm a Rose, so I knew how to fake it, knew how to make someone fall in love with *me*, all that, but… it was abstract. But then I actually kinda liked it, so I ended up sticking around."

"Well… I started writing it for similar reasons."

"And you *still* haven't told me what your pen name is or what your books are."

I rolled my eyes, shaking my head as I started backing toward my room again. "*Fine*," I told her, then offered a name and title that made her mouth drop open.

"DOSH!" she screeched, making my footsteps grind to a halt. "*That* is *you?!* Sis! That latest book! I… I *love* your work," she admitted, bringing a massive smile to my face. "I was halfway ready to stop reading you though, because there was never any sex, but then in the last one, you… oh *ugh*," she groaned, making a face. "Isaiah brought something out of you, didn't he? Ew."

"He's brought a lot out of me, and I've brought a lot out of him," I teased, ignoring her pretend gags as I grabbed what I needed for us to head out the door. In the car, we ended up talking more about my writing, and *her* experience as a reader, and the whole thing was just…. Gratifying. I'd known it was inevitable that the people I loved would find out about the writing. Still, I'd expected it to be a whole embarrassing ordeal.

And instead it just… wasn't.

It actually felt rather good.

We made it to Pen's little apartment right on time to start welcoming guests, and I used my key to let us in. Pen was a stickler for keeping the place spotless, so all we had to do was put out a few decorations and food, and then wait for her boyfriend to give us the signal that she was heading home.

That signal… did not come.

What happened instead was a sudden flinging open of the door. Pen stepped inside, her face streaked with ruined mascara and tears, took one look around and… bursted out crying before she bypassed the space full of people to rush to her room.

I looked at Alicia across the room, and she intuitively knew to come with me to where Pen had thrown herself across the bed.

"Hey," I asked, sitting down beside her to rub soothing circles on her back. "What's going on?"

"I don't want to talk about it." she replied, her words muffled by the pillow she'd buried her face in.

I sighed. "Well… I won't try to force you to, if you don't want to, but I need you to let us know if you're okay. Did something happen with Tyler?"

She pulled her face up from the pillow just long enough to

look back and forth between me and Alicia. "He... he... nevermind," she sobbed. "I *don't* want to talk about it! Can you guys just... everybody leave me alone!"

That made me raise my eyebrows, but... sure.

We'd leave *her* alone.

I motioned for Alicia to come out of the room with me, and we closed the door behind us before I leaned in to tell her, "I'm about to go find Tyler and make him tell me what the fuck is going on. You wanna come?"

"Is that even a real question?" she smirked. "I'm already planning the route in my head."

"You know his address?"

"I know how much his rent is, and that his father pays for it," Alicia laughed. "Of *course* I know his address."

"Okay, well let's go," I told her, walking out into the main area to note that Loren had already cleared the guests out.

"Is she okay?" Loren asked, coming from where she'd just let the last guest out.

Alicia shrugged. "We're about to find out. Can you stay here with her until we get back?"

"Of course," she agreed. "Yaya is with Cree, and my man isn't expecting me until later, so I'm good. Y'all about to ride on somebody?"

"If that's what it takes," I told her, looping an arm through Alicia's, rushing her along. "Let's go."

For some reason, that was amusing to her, but she let me drag her down to the car. It wasn't until we were both inside that she spoke up.

"So... you sure are in a hurry to go question this guy about what he may or may not have done to Pen, huh?"

"Hell yes, I am," I agreed. "I want his fucking head on a platter—did you see how upset she was?!"

"Oh, I get it- trust me," she said, her eyes on the road as she pulled out of the parking spot and started us on the way.

"I'm just… surprised at how extremely protective you're being. I'd think you wanted to step back and let Penelope handle it all on her own, instead of us… smothering her."

I sucked my teeth. "Okay, really? We're doing *this?*"

"I'm not doing anything, I'm saying!" she declared, feigning innocence. "I'm just *honestly* surprised."

"Well, *don't be*," I declared, crossing my arms. "Since this situation is totally different. Pen was upset, and crying, and we don't *really* know this guy, and—"

"She asked us to leave it alone."

"Yes, but—"

"*But* nothing," Alicia interrupted, shaking her head. "It didn't appear that she was physically hurt at all – just upset. And I'm sure that if he'd touched her… she would tell us that. I don't think she would have left it at, *everybody leave me alone.* Not after everything. So… we have a decision ahead of us. We can go smack this dude around, which is – honestly – my preferred approach. *Or*… we can do what she asked – what *you* or *I* would want, if it was either of us. We can leave it alone, and let her handle it how she sees fit. We can just go grab her favorite snacks and whatever else she might want, go back to her place, watch shitty movies and pretend this *Tyler* doesn't even exist. And then if *she* wants us to go kick his ass…"

"I'm getting first lick."

"Of course you would," Alicia agreed, pulling into the parking lot of Tyler's building. "So… what's it gonna be?"

Damn.

On *one* hand… I was more than willing to be out for blood, determined to get it from the man who'd hurt my Penelope, who I saw as a little sister. On the other hand though… she was right. For all my bluster about wanting space to handle my own life without having a protective detail up my ass, when it was somebody *I* cared about in question, I was ready to take Tyler's ass to a black site and pull his teeth out.

So… maybe now I understood a little more where Alicia was coming from.

"Okay, *okay*," I conceded – annoyed about it, but still. "We… should probably wait until Pen wants to talk about it, so we don't step on her toes. I don't want her feeling like we just steamroll her life, instead of listening to her."

Alicia's top lip curled. "Eh. I still say let's bust his kneecaps now, ask questions later, but… I'm willing to defer to you. Glad you can practice what you preach, little sister."

I chuckled. "Yeah. Barely."

"Let's get out of here," she said, reaching for the gear shift just as my phone chimed with a text.

"Hold on," I told her, tapping into the message to see that it was from Tyler.

"How is Pen? I'm leaving my place right now to come check on her, if that's okay?" – Pen's boo Tyler."

Sure enough, just a few seconds after I finished reading that, the building's front door opened, and he came jogging out.

We didn't even have to think about it.

Alicia and I both hopped out, catching up to Tyler before he could make it to his own vehicle.

"What do you mean, *how is Pen?*" I asked, walking right into his face as he tried to back away from me, until he was pinned against his car. "You tell *me*, how she is. You were supposed to be with her, bringing her to the party, but she's at her place crying her eyes out. What did you do?"

A few feet away, Alicia stood smirking—probably over the fact that we'd completely abandoned our plan to *not* do this.

"I didn't do anything!" Tyler insisted—believably. "We were just… we were upstairs, and we were…" his light brown skin flushed a bit redder with youthful shame that contradicted his stature and strong, defined facial features. "She… had these scars, that I could feel. So I just asked her, if she'd been in an accident or something. I thought it was a simple question, but she freaked out on me, and ran out. Then she freaked out *more* when I caught her, so… I let her leave. Maybe I shouldn't have. Because now she's not answering the phone, and y'all are here looking like some kinda assassins or something, but I swear—I did nothing to hurt her. Not intentionally."

Oh.

Oh.

Shit.

The scars in question were the result of a sadistic client, from Pen's time as a Rose. The very scars she'd come to me about a few weeks ago, wanting to get my input about using tattoos to have them covered.

It was sensitive to her, and with good reason—for reasons *exactly* like this. It was much easier to explain a tattoo than to make up a story for the scars—the easier option over telling the truth. Part of getting the ink was so she could reclaim the acts of intimacy that the wounds made awkward. I knew she liked this guy a lot though, so… maybe she'd thought it would be fine.

That *she'd* be fine.

And maybe she *had* been fine.

Until she wasn't.

"She's upset," I told Tyler, backing up to give him some space—and ease his fear that I might put a blade in his gut. "It's not my place to talk about her business, but I can say… it's a tough topic for her. So you may have to give her a little time. Are you willing to do that?"

"Whatever she needs," Tyler assured, immediately. "I like Pen, a *lot*. I didn't mean to upset her. I was just curious. I don't have to ask about them, and she doesn't have to tell me anything she doesn't want me to know."

I nodded. "Okay. So… I don't think you should go to her

place. Unless she tells you she wants that. I will tell her you
wanted to though, and that you're sorry she's upset."

"Thank you. Can you… can you give her this too?" he
asked, handing me a gift bag I hadn't even realized was in his
hand. "I was going to give it to her before I brought her to the
party, but everything kinda…"

"Went south," I filled in for him, accepting the bag. "Yeah.
I'll give it to her."

Alicia and I went back to the car, and Tyler went back
upstairs – we didn't pull off until he'd gone inside.

"He seems like a decent kid," Alicia murmured as she
merged into traffic. "Why couldn't you get yourself a nice
normal boyfriend like that?"

I sucked my teeth. "Says the woman practically married to
a cop."

"*Former* cop," she corrected. "And either would be better
than a non-reformed Thorn."

"Oh *God*, I thought we were past this," I said. "When are
you going to just *accept* that me and Isaiah are a thing, and
gonna continue to be?"

"Every time I try, I remember that he's a Thorn. And not a
Wilder kinda thorn either."

I huffed. "You act like Wilder wasn't a killer too – like *you*
weren't," I reminded her, making her cringe.

"I'd be just as concerned if you told me you were dating a
Rose – it's not specific to Isaiah," she said, as if that made it
better. "I just… *know* Wilder now. And I was wary of him at
first too."

"I get that, but *I* know Isaiah."

"Like I thought I knew Reo Tanaka?"

"*Seriously*?!" I sputtered. "Alicia, Reo was a psychopath and
everybody *knew* it about him. It's not fair to act like he's the
standard for all Thorns."

"Except he *is* the standard for all Thorns," Alicia

countered. "He was the ideal. Don't let the fact that some of them appear well-adjusted make you forget that. They – *we* – were literally bred to be charming, ruthless… maniacs. And they did a good job."

"Well, thank goodness for therapy," I said, not giving in to her assertion. "Yes, we all know the power of conditioning, but we also know none of that is final. Every single one of us is living proof of that – some have just been in the healing process longer than others."

She raised an eyebrow at me. "So… are you telling me Isaiah is in therapy?"

"Not that it's your business, but… yes. He started last week. He hates it, but… he's trying. And that, to me, is a good enough place for now. And the fact that he makes me happy, should be good enough for you."

Alicia shook her head. "Nope. That *isn't* good enough for me," she said. "But… the fact that he's actively working on himself, which lowers the chances that I'll have to kill his ass over you? Well… that's a gamechanger."

I laughed. "Can I consider that your blessing?"

She peeked over at me from the driver's seat, just before we pulled into the store parking lot.

"Okay. Fine."

twelve

I FELT LIKE SHIT.

And as much as I wished it weren't self-imposed, I had no one to blame but myself for the crabby mood and sleepless nights, leading to *worse* moods.

All because at some unidentifiable point, some switch in my brain had flipped, and things were – ridiculously, I knew – *too* good.

That proverbial "other shoe" was bound to drop at any moment.

Right?

Right?

I was so sure it had me on edge, constantly looking for signs something was wrong, so it wouldn't catch me by surprise.

Which, of course, wasn't helping the mood, or the ability to rest.

Or hell—maybe *this* was it.

I was so paranoid about something going wrong that I couldn't just enjoy it anymore, so I was going to worry myself to death.

"Why are you looking so stressed?" Pen whispered from beside me in our seats on the plane, snuggling deeper under the plush blankets we'd been provided. "You're blowing the vibe."

I rolled my eyes, even though she couldn't see it with *hers* closed. "Sorry," I muttered, not bothering to force my tone into anything other than sarcastic and dry.

Even though... I *was* kinda blowing the vibe.

This was supposed to be a good time, *especially* for Pen. That whole thing on her birthday had been a setback, and even though she'd recovered quickly and still had Tyler wrapped around her finger... I knew she was still struggling.

This trip was supposed to help with that.

Finally, we were making our way to the Heights to get that tattoo she so desperately wanted, along with a needed break from Vegas. As exciting as it was from the perspective of people dropping in to visit for a few days at a time, living there was... probably the same as living anywhere else, honestly.

After a while, you just needed to see something different.

So, we found ourselves on a private flight arranged by Alicia. With our father's fortune in our hands now, we didn't *need* to borrow the Whitfield jet, but there had been some gentle insistence. I was happy to redistribute *that* money into the charity anyway, and take advantage of the offer, so it all worked out.

Pen was going to get her tattoo, we were going to get to see Tempest, it should've been happy times. But instead of relaxing into the butter-soft leather seats and taking a much-needed nap, like Pen, I found myself with my mind reeling, and always coming back to this one particular worry.

Whether Zay would still be there when I got back.

Again, ridiculous.

Probably.

That man *loved* me.

But...

He'd been... distant.

Well.

Not *distant*, exactly, just always in his head, like he was mentally a million miles away. There was never an issue of him treating me like a bother, or being any less engaged when I had his attention. Something with him was just... off.

And obviously I couldn't just *talk* to him about it—What was I supposed to say?

Hey, you've been just as attentive as always, you're a great boyfriend, you seem to be in a better place, but I don't like that you have private thoughts that you're thinking around me sometimes and aren't telling me everything happening in your head.

That might just drive him not even *further* away.

Just away, period.

When I'd asked if something was wrong, he'd given me the *least* satisfying possible answer.

"Something wrong? Nah, nothing's **wrong.***"*

Goddamn semantics.

Maybe nothing was wrong, but something was definitely *up*.

And because I didn't want to push, after I'd already pushed – and won – about him going to therapy, I didn't want to test my luck.

So I just wondered.

About all the things that could be the problem.

Was he depressed?

Was he bored?

Did he need to kill somebody?

Had he killed somebody?

Was he sick of me?

Was I hindering his progress because of our past?

I'd been so concerned about the possibility of my therapist telling me he wasn't good for me, but it had never occurred to me that just maybe... I wasn't good for *him*.

What if?

What if?!

Girl.

You're doing the most right now.

I blew out a sigh, forcing myself to think about something

—*anything*—else before I induced a fucking panic attack. Instead, I spent the bulk of the flight writing out a whole other story outline, different from the one Alicia had found weeks ago.

That one was pretty much done.

It was amazing how rapidly that story had unfolded for me once I sat down and got started. I was probably going to make readers mad all over again for the shift in content, tone, and heat level, but ultimately… I was going to write whatever came to me.

By the time we landed, I had my new thing figured out, and had accomplished *not* spending those hours with Isaiah filling my head. That put me in a much better mental space to meet up with Tempest, who picked us up from the airport and drive us to our hotel. This was our time to freshen up, eat, and decompress before the meeting with Pen's tattoo artist— Tempest's boyfriend, Tristan.

"You are like a whole other person," I gushed at Temp, running my fingers through the long braids she was currently rocking. "Who would've thought we would find you in anything but all black, and those damn boots. Look at you in a *green* sweater," I teased as she batted my hand away.

"I just tossed it on—no big deal," she insisted.

"Oh, I beg to differ. That you even have it is telling me a lot."

"Enough about me—tell me a *lot* about you and Isaiah, how about that," she said, glancing at Pen, who was busy taking selfies out on the balcony. "You're not moved in together yet? Hell, married? You're up under him every time I call you."

"Not *every* time."

"Fine—*most* times," Tempest laughed. "Is that the only part you can deny?"

"I can deny all of it, because I don't even know what we're doing, so we're *certainly* not moving in together."

"But you're still always up under that nigga," she laughed, just as my phone started ringing. "I bet that's him right now."

Of course it was.

And as soon as I saw his name on the screen, I remembered that I was supposed to have called him as soon as Pen and I landed, but in the excitement of seeing Tempest, I'd forgotten.

"Hey," I answered. "We're fine. Sorry I forgot to call."

"Damn right," he chuckled. "You know I was willing and ready to hop a flight myself if you hadn't answered."

I grinned, ignoring Tempest's silent, distracting teasing. "Yes, I know. What are you doing instead of flying across the country to save me from unspoken danger now?"

"Just chilling," he answered, at about the same time as a female voice sounded in the background.

"What are you doing, Zay?!" she asked, and I felt my face immediately grow hot.

Just chilling my ass.

"I'm on the phone, Tam."

His answer was completely neutral, and answered the question on my mind of who the hell he was with.

Tamra.

His "friend".

"*Hiiiii Deeeee!*" she squealed in the background, making me angry even though her tone was playful. I knew they were friends, sure, but…

"Will you stop?" he scolded her, and she said something back that I couldn't make out. "Sorry," he told me. "Tamra's silly ass."

"You two hanging out again?" I asked, hoping it didn't sound as pitiful as it felt.

"Yeah, with Wilder and a few others. Grabbing lunch before we head to do this thing at the Cartwright center with Cree."

"Okay. Well… have fun," I told him, only feeling *slightly* better knowing he wasn't with just Tamra. I'd never really thought to be jealous before, but with him acting weird lately anyway… it was hard not to wonder.

And that must've been pretty clear on my face, based on the way Tempest questioned me once we were off the phone.

"You know I've had to deal with the "*friend*" too," she said, after I explained the situation. "Problem here is, I don't know if you can beat Tamra's ass. She's a Rose."

"I'm not interested in even trying," I laughed. "I don't even know if there's anything there. They're friends. They've *been* friends."

"Which there's nothing wrong with that… if that's all it is. *Is* that all it is?"

"Is what all what is?" Pen asked, finally stepping in from the balcony.

"Grown folks' business," Temp countered, words that Pen rolled her eyes over, but I appreciated—I *loved* Pen, but I really didn't need her barely-older-than-teenaged optimism right now.

I needed to be real.

Instead of letting me dwell on the situation like I wanted to, Tempest took Pen and I to *Wax Poetic*, the candle shop she'd opened when she moved to the Heights. There, I immersed myself in the sights and scents of her new products before she ushered us along to get lunch at the same soul food spot she'd taken me when I visited months ago, and then to Urban Grind to just soak up the warm energy before it was time for Pen's appointment.

"Dacia!" Tristan greeted me with a hug when we arrived. "You're still feeling your ink, right? No buyer's remorse?"

I wrinkled my nose at him. "*Hell* no, of course not," I said. "It's flawless—why else do you think we brought the kid?"

The kid being Penelope, of course, who was suddenly

nervous about it, now that it was time for the moment of truth. And really, it only took a bit to get her to relax and loosen up, with Tristan talking her through the ink colors and all that, helping her understand every step, the aftercare, and whatever else she might need to know.

And then... it was time to start.

Tristan's work was fast, but impeccable, buoyed by him already having pictures as a reference for what he would be doing. Because it was a large scale coverup, it was vital for him to know what he was working with ahead of time, to formulate his plan and the design for what Pen wanted.

Beautiful sprays of daffodils to cover every scar and symbolize what we'd all needed—new beginnings.

A chance to not be so beholden to the reality the *Garden* had tried to impose on us.

For Pen, it wasn't so much about the rose tattoo—she wasn't that bothered by it. Those scars, though, they held the bulk of the trauma holding her back. I knew that getting inked would work for her the way it had worked for Tempest.

It would be transformative.

For me... I was realizing that the ink didn't matter at all.

There was so much *other* trauma, so much additional baggage, that even though the tattoo was covered, even though my life was completely changed, even though I had everything I thought I wanted... I still didn't believe I deserved it.

I *still* didn't believe this could be my life without it all going terribly wrong.

The thought plagued me for the rest of the trip, like some fucked-up self-fulfilling prophecy. I was so worried about losing it all that I couldn't even have a good time—even though I did a superb job of pretending.

. . .

BACK IN VEGAS, my mental state didn't improve, which only made me *more* frustrated.

I knew what my therapist would say, because she'd already said it. I knew what Alicia would say, what Pen would say, what Loren would say, hell… I even knew what *Cree* would say.

You deserve to be happy, just lean into it.

Except… *did I?*

"What are you so preoccupied with?" Zay asked, pulling me from my thoughts. We were at his place for a change, instead of always being at mine. Instead of absorbing anything happening in the movie we were watching, I was… overthinking myself into a bad mood.

"Wow – *you're* accusing *me* of being preoccupied? That's funny," I snapped, pulling myself up from the couch.

I didn't get far with him right behind me, grabbing my hand to get me to turn around. "Uh… you wanna tell me what *that's* about?" he asked, brows furrowed in confusion.

"What's there to be confused about?" I asked. "You've been in your head at every opportunity for damn near a month, but you want to accuse me of being preoccupied. It's just bold."

His expression softened. "Dee… I—"

"I asked you if anything was wrong. You said no. But that never felt quite like the truth. And it seems like you've been spending all this extra time with Tamra lately…"

"Tamra is my friend – yes, I spend time with her."

"Is that really all she is?"

His confused expression pulled deeper. "What?! *Yes.* That's all it is – all it's *ever* been."

"So you've never been intimate with her?" I pressed. "After you broke my heart, and you went on to become a big bad Thorn, and made "friends" with the big bad Rose… you're telling me you and her… *never?*"

He pushed out a sigh that said… everything.

"If I said there was nothing, that would be a lie," he finally spoke, even though I already felt numb. "But… Dee… you *know* how that went – you know what we were. We all just did the job."

"Fucking her was the job?"

"*No.* Never that far, but… we've played a couple before. More than once. For the job. And internally, it was awkward as fuck, because it wasn't *like that* with us." He stopped speaking to shake his head. "Where is this even coming from?"

"It's coming from *you*, being *different* lately," I answered. "What else am I supposed to think, when it seems like if you're not with me, you're with her, and you've been all quiet and contemplative, and telling me nothing's wrong! I always thought this thing, you coming back to me, was too good to be true. So I wish you'd just… stop dragging it out."

"Stop dragging… Dee, have you *lost your mind?*" he asked, with more grit than I was expecting so suddenly. "What do you think is about to happen? I'm gonna… what, leave you to be with Tamra?"

"Are you?"

"*No*," he insisted, dragging me up against him. "What is it going to take for you to believe that shit can just… be okay? We were fine – *you* were fine – and now you're switching up on me. What the hell is going on?"

I tried to get out of his hold, but that clearly wasn't happening. So I just glared at him instead.

"You're right. I *was* fine. But then *you* started being weird, and I started worrying, and once I started worrying, it just… spiraled."

He sighed. "Well… unfurl, damn." He took a step back, scrubbing a hand over his face. "You can't jump to worst-case scenario every time I've got something heavy on my mind."

"How about you tell me what's going on, so I don't have a reason to?"

"*Fuck*," he muttered. "I was still trying to figure out how I felt about the shit before I told you, but... I talked to your sister's people, about the DNA tests or whatever. To find out where I'm from. I didn't tell you at first because I wasn't sure I was going to do it, but Tam thought it was a good idea."

"Right."

"Don't do that shit," he warned, and I pressed my lips closed, waiting on him to finish. "Yes, I talked to her about it, but not you—because she's closer to my experience, of not knowing. You have your family, *right* now. You know your history. And... just honestly, she and I have a history that you and I don't. So... I talked to my *friend* about this. And she encouraged me to do it, and I did it. And I've been on edge about it, and maybe you felt that. But I didn't want to burden you with it, when you've been on edge yourself. Then the results came. And... I got contact info, and all that. But I still didn't—*don't*—know what I'm going to do with it. So... that's what's been on my mind."

I just... stood there for a bit, with my lips parted, before I shook my head. "What do you mean, you don't know what you're going to do? You're not going to reach out?"

"I mean exactly that," he said, turning to walk away, with me following. "They don't know me, and I don't know them—what the fuck am I supposed to say?"

I nodded. "Right. Well... where are they? *Who* are they?"

He grabbed a glass from the cabinet, filling it with water and taking a drink before he answered. "Israel. And Ethiopia. Apparently, I'm the son of foreign service officers—diplomats. They were killed, at a conference. Suspicious circumstances I'll probably never get proper answers about. According to what I found, I was in the car too, but was pulled from the wreckage, no injuries. And then... I just disappeared."

"My goodness," I whispered, pressing my hands to my chest. "I... I'm sorry you won't have a chance to know them.

And... I'm sorry to have made you feel you couldn't tell me this before."

He frowned. "Dee... you have nothing to be sorry about. It wasn't so much that I couldn't tell you, I just... I didn't want to burden you with it. You were knee deep in writing your book, and you helping Pen, and then you had your trip. There was nothing you could do to change any of it, so I didn't see the point of putting it in your lap."

"The point would've been you not having to carry the weight of that by yourself!"

Except...

Right.

He *wasn't*.

Because Tamra knew.

That realization must've been written all over my face, because Zay put his glass down and started toward me.

"Hey," he said, stepping in the way of me leaving the kitchen before he cupped my face in his hands. "Let's not turn this into something it doesn't have to be."

I forced a smile to my lips. "I hear you, but... easier said than done. And I think... maybe we need some space?"

"No."

My eyebrows went up. "No?"

"That's what I said, Dee," he shrugged. "I don't need any space. And *you* don't need any either – you just want me to agree with whatever sabotage you have going on right now, and I'm not doing it."

"Excuse me?"

"I was clear. As fuck," he added, his gaze not wavering from mine. "I'll cop to being preoccupied, because I *have* had a lot on my mind. Now how about you tell me what's up with *you*?"

My eyes narrowed. "What? There's nothing *up* with me."

"Dee, you were bubbly and starry-eyed, couldn't get

enough of me just a few weeks ago. Now you're talking about needing *space*. You really expect me to believe there's nothing up?"

"*You* just admitted to being distant."

"Stop deflecting," he countered. "You think I haven't noticed you're not sleeping? Barely eating. Moody…"

"So we're going to blame all this on… what, my period starting?"

"Shit, I don't know, but baby… *something* is up," he said, in a soothing tone as his hands planted at my waist, pulling me into him. "Maybe I'm wrong – maybe this is just a normal valley, and we just haven't been on the same wavelength and need to pull back together. I'm good with doing that – *I want to do that*. But I also want you to consider that…"

"*I'm* the problem?"

"I didn't say that," he quickly corrected. "I'm not absolving myself of needing to communicate better, or any of that. I think we've both been off, and we can both do better with just… saying what we need to say. Instead of assuming how the other might feel?"

I pushed out a breath, then nodded. "I… I can agree with that," I told him, and then welcomed the press of his lips to mine.

"Good. Now… about Tamra…"

I rolled my eyes. "Fine. She's your friend."

"Nah," he chuckled. "That's not good enough. It obviously has been bothering you, so… why don't you come out with us one night. Hell, *tonight*," he suggested. "So you can see just how much she is not checking for me like that."

"Okay, but are *you* checking for *her*?"

I let out a squeal as Isaiah grabbed me by the ass, using his hold there to lift me up onto the counter.

"Is that *really* even a question?"

Was it?

Was it?

… no.

Not really.

Still, it *felt* like a question, and it made sense in my head, even with nothing but paranoia to support it.

I *wanted* to know better than to think he wanted anybody except me. And at the moment, instead of hesitating… I went with that feeling.

"No. Not at all."

SO, we didn't go out with them *that* night.

Instead, the "double date" Isaiah proposed happened several nights later—a completely informal event that found us in a mostly empty bar, well past closing.

They knew the owner or something.

I'd known Tamra and Wilder before Isaiah came back into my life—not from the Garden, but from their work with Alicia. They were both officially on the payroll of the security firm she'd built, as some kind of counterbalance to what she used to be.

It seemed to be working for her.

It seemed to work for all of them, really.

Wilder had been one of the first Thorns to show up—one of the first to convert. His crush on Alicia had been so obvious, to where I thought he and Cree might end up throwing blows. Not that Alicia ever encouraged it—I wasn't even sure she *noticed*. But maybe Cree talked to him or something, because Wilder fell back, and then… Tamra came into the picture, and Wilder had to chase her.

And now… they were a couple.

She didn't—wouldn't—say so, because she was on her free-spirit thing, and he wouldn't say it because she didn't want to, but… they were. I didn't know either of them *well* though, had never engaged more than a few words of conversation. So although I understood that she was coupled with Wilder, that fact told me nothing about whether she *wanted* Isaiah.

She answered that question with her mannerisms.

At one point during the night, Isaiah had pulled me aside, asking why I was so quiet. My response focused on being fatigued, which I was, after working out with Alicia that morning and then spending all day at the computer. So it wasn't a lie.

It just wasn't the whole reason.

I was quiet because I was observing—years of neglect had made me rusty, but reading people had always been a decent skill of mine. I was certainly not at the same level I'd been when predicting the client was the highest thing on my priority list, but I was *watching* Tamra.

The way she interacted with Isaiah—the way she spoke to him, laughed at his jokes, touched him, looked at him, all of it. And I compared it all to how she was with Wilder.

By the time we made it to that empty bar, I'd arrived at a conclusion I was incredibly sure of.

I was... maybe... kinda... tripping.

Tamra didn't shy away from interacting with Isaiah in front of me—which would have been suspicious, really. She punched his shoulder when he teased her, slapped his leg when he made her laugh, gave him her full attention when he was speaking, all that. With Wilder, though... all her touches *lingered*. She leaned into him, undressed him with her eyes, bit her lip sometimes when he was talking—all subtle. It was pronounced to me because I was *looking* for it, but it wasn't like she was putting on a show.

She was just *attracted* to Wilder, and was very clearly going to screw his brains out once they were alone again after this date was over.

And seeing that for myself made the idea of anything different just seem... silly.

"I'm glad Zay talked you into coming out with us – I was starting to think you didn't like me or something," Tamra teased. She and I were alone at the bar, watching Wilder and Isaiah shit-talk each other at a nearby pool table.

I grabbed my half-melted sprite, and took a long drink, trying to wet my throat. "It… it wasn't *that*, exactly. More like I didn't want to get in the way."

She wasn't talking about the more recent thing of me wondering if she was more than just friends with Isaiah – this wasn't the first time I'd been invited out with a group of former Roses and Thorns. I'd always felt disconnected from their group – the killers – and I didn't want my awkwardness or uncertainty keeping Isaiah from making the connections he needed.

But… maybe if I'd come out sooner, I wouldn't have ever wondered about anything between her and Zay.

"*You?*" Tamra sucked here teeth. "How could *you* be in the way, when you're the one who even brought him into the fold in the first place?"

I raised an eyebrow. "Huh?"

"I ran into Isaiah in this *very* bar months and months ago. Right when I'd first found out about what Alicia was trying to do here. I… had agreed to join her. And I asked Isaiah to join too, so he wouldn't be out in the cold. He turned me down. But then *you* suggest it, and… here he is. So if anything, I should be thanking you."

I almost choked on a piece of ice. "*Thanking* me? For what?"

"For bringing my friend back," she said, like it should've been obvious. "Zay and I practically… grew up together, I guess. He's like a brother to me. And I was worried about his ass. Like… a *lot*. But you managed to convince him to be a part of the group, instead of doing God-knows-what out on his own. Not to mention… *girl*. Therapy?! Good luck to getting a normal man to go, but a *Thorn*? We've gotta get you on the hostage negotiation team or something, you can talk a person into anything."

Laughing, I shook my head. "I... I don't think I talked him into anything that wasn't already there, you know? Like the desire was already present, he just needed the right little push. For instance... you talking him into doing the DNA test thing. He didn't even really talk to me about that, until it was done. Hell – until he had the results."

Tamra sighed. "I told him that was a bad idea."

"What?"

"Not talking to you about it. He insisted that he didn't want to "burden" you with it, but... I didn't think you would see it like that."

"I wouldn't have."

She smirked, picking up her glass to raise in my direction. "See? If they would just believe we know what we're talking about *every* time instead of just sometimes."

"I'll drink to that," I chuckled, tapping my glass to hers before my gaze fell on the guys again. "I... get why he didn't, though. This freedom, this knowledge, all of it. It's all still pretty new."

Tamra nodded. "Yeah. And it's hard to process. Like, I went through the whole ordeal of hunting down my people, you know? And I found them. But... what I found wasn't a fucking fairytale, you know? So as much as you're gaining something from knowing, you might also end up happening upon a loss. And that shit is like a punch to the gut. But I know I'm preaching to the choir here..."

Yeah.

She was.

I understood *exactly* what she meant, about the simultaneous increase and loss.

Being in the Garden came with an understanding that

you'd lost something—you just didn't know what. It stayed at the fringes of your mind and you left it there, because it hurt too much to explore.

But then… by some stroke of luck—named Alicia—we were able to reclaim what was taken from us. The thing with that was… depending on your situation, you may have been better off not knowing.

Yes, I'd gained a sister, and her family, and our father's fortune. But that increase came knowing that my father was gone, and that his death had been arranged by my mother's hand.

It came with knowing that I was only in the Garden in the first place because my own mother had made it so, and *kept* me there. Every abuse, every indignity I suffered… it was because I didn't matter to her.

And *that*?

That fucking stung.

So… yeah.

I got it.

But there was never a time when I wished I *didn't* know the truth.

"Good thing we can choose our families, huh?" I said, and Tamra smiled at me before she nodded.

"Yeah. It really is." She took a sip from her drink, saying nothing for a long moment, and then, "I'm happy I didn't kill Wilder when I had the chance."

I bursted out laughing at that, so loud that it drew the guys' attention. From Isaiah's smile, I could tell he was glad to see Tamra and I getting along, since that was kinda the whole point of this.

I broke away from his gaze to look at her. "Yeah, that would've made it pretty hard to be together."

"Right?" she giggled. "I guess it's a good thing neither of

us holds grudges either—cause we were definitely kicking each other's asses."

My eyes went wide. "So… that whole thing about him chasing you… you guys were full blown *fighting*, huh?"

"Oh *yeah*," she confirmed. "I maintain that he only caught me because… well, I guess that doesn't matter, so let me stop before I get mad thinking about it," she laughed. "But yeah. And now… he's my favorite sparring partner. The sex after is amazing."

"Love that for you," I laughed, raising my glass to her again.

She tapped hers to it, then emptied her drink down her throat. "You know… I used to tease the life out of Zay about you," she said, making my eyebrows shoot up.

"Really?"

"Yes, really. When he and I met, he'd been off your guard duty for a year or so, but… you were the first personal thing he ever told me about. Hell – the *only* personal thing, because… what else would there have been? I was actually kinda jealous of you," she admitted. "Not like, because I wanted Zay – he was always fine, but also *eww*. Anyway, it was more like… I never had any *security*, I didn't get personal attention from any Thorns, you know?"

I smirked. "Yeah, I get it, but… you also got to be strong, you know? You got to be fierce, and *feared*, and kick people's asses. While *I*…"

"Yeah," she nodded, dropping her head. "I know."

"And you know what's crazy? When I got… "pulled from the field", to teach hair and makeup for the other Roses instead… that was almost worse. Because even though I didn't have to do that anymore, I felt complicit. Like I was sending these girls into a nightmare."

Tamra huffed. "You say that like you had a choice. You were – we *all* were – programmed to stay in line. Maybe if the consequences were just death, that was one thing. But we all know… there's worse."

"Yeah, and I found out the hard way, didn't I?" I said, rolling a stray piece of ice from my glass around in my mouth. "I was so stupid. But I needed to know what had happened to Pen, and I—"

"You were human. You actually gave a fuck about somebody, and there's nothing stupid in that. Well… I won't say that, but… it's nothing to be ashamed of, at least."

"Right."

Tamra let out a sigh and shook her head. "I don't think I've ever known Zay to be as… *man*, he was *irate* when he found out you were missing. And not just mad, either, you know? He was… distraught. Because he'd been checking up on you. Keeping up with you, all that time. I don't believe he ever let go of that dream of y'all being together, even though he didn't think it would really happen. He didn't believe that kind of good fortune would happen to him. But as long as you were okay, he was okay. And then when you weren't…. he was *not*."

"He… never told me that," I whispered. "I mean, I knew that he'd watched me over the years, he said that. But him not being okay…"

"Yeah, he was… just a different person. Completely unrestrained. And the Garden *loved* it. I was scared for him though, because he wasn't… it was like he didn't care if he died. Then the Garden fell, and I just had no idea what happened to him. Even when we ran into each a few months ago, he was… he was calmer, less aggressive, but still not… *my brother.* Now though… look at him *laughing*, and having a good time, and just… happy. Because he finally got his princess."

Whew.

When we came out for this "date", it had been solely to cure my ridiculous jealousy. And the thing was… there was never *really* a doubt to me that Isaiah loved me. We'd talked around it often, while never directly saying the words to each other, but still… I *knew*.

I don't think I understood the depth of it, though.

And now that I did?

I felt even sillier for being worried about Tamra.

It was evident to me that she loved him too, but in precisely the way she said, exactly as he himself had maintained—a brother. And instead of being jealous of that close connection, hearing her story made me glad they'd had each other, instead of being plagued with loneliness like I had.

I… was grateful for her.

I opened my mouth to express that to her, but what came out instead was an embarrassingly big yawn.

"Damn girl," Tamra laughed. "Do we need to get you home?"

"No, I'm totally fine."

"Sis, if you're sleepy, you can really just say that," she giggled. "Zay, come take your girl home before she passes out over here," she called, and I covered my face.

Instantly it seemed, Zay was beside me, wrapping an arm around my shoulder. "Hey, you okay?"

"I'm *fine*," I laughed. "I yawned, that's all. You know I've been burning the midnight oil over this book."

"Unnecessarily," he agreed. "So you're gonna sleep in tomorrow, get some rest."

"What if I don't want to do that?"

"It's a good thing I didn't ask what you *wanted*," he countered, helping me up. "Come on."

"Do you see what you've caused?" I asked Tamra as Wilder hooked an arm around her waist too.

"Girl let that man put you to sleep," she teased. "I'm about to do the same," she said, turning up to Wilder just as he lowered his head to kiss her.

None of us lingered after that.

It was clear what Tamra and Wilder were about to get into, and I really was tired, so I didn't argue any further about going home. After a hot, shared shower, and a little snack, my bed was calling my name, and I was more than happy to welcome Isaiah into it with me.

"So… what's the verdict?" he asked, getting right up close to pull me into him. "You still thinking about that cage match with Tamra over me?"

"*No*," I laughed. "I… am firmly planted in my senses now."

"Good to know," he chuckled, leaning in to kiss me. "Now… get some sleep."

"I will. But first I've gotta tell you something."

He raised an eyebrow at me. "What's that?"

"I love you."

A slow, confused grin spread over his mouth. "I… love you too. But that's not… news to you, is it?"

I shook my head. "Nope. Just making sure."

fourteen

UGH.

What is that smell?

Trouble focusing during my morning writing session had driven me to put headphones on, filling my conscious with white noise. I'd shifted gears, instead returning to my ongoing email thread with Rowan Phillips about the re-entry program I wanted to bring to the Cartwright center. Assistance with housing, mental health, education, healthcare – and whatever else other young trafficking survivors might need to establish real freedom.

Especially as I came to a place of my own, this was paramount for me.

So I was working.

The blotting out of any distractions had paved the way for me to be productive, but it also made me quite easy to sneak up on.

I had no idea Isaiah was there.

Well… until I smelled him.

Based on the odor he was putting off, the sight of him in sweat-drenched athletic clothes was no surprise.

"Hey," I greeted, entirely distracted from my work now that he was pulling his shirt off. "I wasn't expecting you until later."

"Yeah, my bad for the interruption," he said, stepping over to where I was seated at the bedroom desk this time – my front office space was too damn comfortable. "We're finishing up a tournament at the center, so the showers were crowded over there. Your place is closer to there than mine."

"It's fine," I told him from behind my hand, covering my nose. "You *need* a shower, so please, have at it."

A playful frown crossed his face before he leaned in, grabbing my ponytail to keep me still as he planted a sloppy kiss on my lips while I tried to squirm away.

"*Ewwww!*" I screeched, my disgust overshadowed by my inability to *not* giggle at his antics. "Zay, you *smell.*"

"You love it," he teased, making me frown, and fully stand up to get away from him. "Ah yeah. Come 'ere girl."

"*No!*" I screeched – again, muted by laughter as he wrapped his sweaty arms around me. I couldn't even be *adequately* appalled by his mustiness with his lips all over my neck, planting kisses everywhere he could reach. "You *stiiiink!*"

"I thought you liked me smelly, my bad," he chuckled, finally releasing me so I could catch my breath. "You know… since you're on a break anyway—"

"I'm not on a break, you interrupted me!"

"What's the difference, princess?" he asked, raising an eyebrow. "Either way, you're not working, so… you may as well come help me get clean… you know, since I *stiiiink*," he teased in a high pitch that was supposed to mimic mine. "Come do something about it."

I *wanted* to turn down that offer.

Especially since he smelled really, *really*, *extra* bad today, after spending the morning helping Cree facilitate a youth basketball tournament at the center. I was proud of him, truly, and *happy* for him that he was finding things that aligned with what he'd always wanted. Sure, those professional basketball dreams were out of reach for him now, but maybe he could still do what he loved in a different way.

But… the whole *finding new dreams to reach* thing was kind of a turn-on.

As was his removal of his boxers.

"You coming? And… *coming*?" he teased, and…

Shit.

Yes.

Yes, I was.

"Get under the water *immediately*," I fussed, making him laugh as he climbed in and turned on the hot spray.

I actually took my time getting undressed—and popping back over to my computer to make sure my progress was saved—before I actually joined him.

Giving him a few minutes to himself to get the funk off first.

Luckily, that worked well, and he was well-immersed in my nose-approved favorite bodywash of his, the one he kept stocked in my bathroom because he knew I liked it.

"*Mmmm*," I groaned, practically melting into him as he welcomed me into his arms.

This was good.

And so were his lips, and his tongue, immediately seeking access to my mouth, which I readily gave. We'd both been so busy that moments like this had been a little hard to find. I had a deadline, and he probably needed to be back at the center sooner than later, but… whatever.

Everything else could wait.

I quickly realized we were both on the same page, when instead of immediately going for penetration… Isaiah kissed his way down my body, until he was on his knees in front of me. He hiked one of my thighs up over his shoulder, urging me to press my back against the smooth tile wall for stability.

I knew what was coming, but… *still.*

I wasn't ready.

His mouth on my clit was perfectly, deliciously… *hot.* The

rasp of his tongue on my hyper-sensitive skin, the thickness of his fingers as he pushed them inside me... *shit.*

Why did it all feel so brand new?

My fingers slid over the wet, super-short coils of his hair, trying in vain to find something to grip. My eyes shut tight, my head pressed back against the hard stone wall as he explored my pussy with his fingers and tongue, somehow discovering new depths... or heights... valleys... whatever.

It was just... *good.*

So good that when my knees unexpectedly bucked in pleasure, I didn't even have the presence of mind to *try* to keep myself up – it was all Isaiah, both of his arms locked around my thighs, oblivious to the wild bucking of my hips as he devoured me until I was just... fully drained.

As soon as he let my thigh down from his shoulder, I sank to the shower floor with him. I cupped his face in my hands, but he acted before my orgasm-addled mind could, kissing me first.

"Seemed like you enjoyed that," he murmured against my lips when he pulled back from the kiss, leaving me breathless.

I snaked a hand between us, wrapping a hand around his dick to squeeze. "Seemed like you did too. Sit back," I insisted, and he lifted an eyebrow at me, but did it, bracing his back against the shower wall.

So I could ride him.

"This floor is hard—" he protested as I straddled him, once he realized what I was doing.

"I don't care," I countered, sinking onto him. I kissed him to stop any further dissent, knowing that once he was fully ensconced in my pussy he wouldn't have any more objections.

"*Shit,*" he groaned into my mouth as our hips connected, and I stayed right there, letting gravity pull us further together.

I agreed with the sentiment.

His hands went to my ass, gripping and squeezing as I

clenched around him, helping my body adjust to him all over again.

My fingers dug into his shoulders as I started to move, just rolling my hips at first, in slow, controlled grind. He retook my mouth as I rode him, his tongue dancing against mine, punctuated with our groans of pleasure.

He was right – the floor was hard.

But that was fine – it kept me grounded, and focused on making us *both* feel good. Even with the bite of the slick tile against my knees, it was so easy – *too* easy – to get absolutely lost in the sensory bliss of him filling me up, over and over again.

Especially once he started moving too, his hands planted at my waist as he met me stroke for stroke in the steam-filled shower, neither of us caring about the steady patter of the water against us. Eventually, one of his hands moved to go between my legs, turning up the dial on my pleasure with his fingers on my clit. The other hand went to my neck, pulling me in again for another kiss as that steady-building pressure in my core threatened to finally bubble over.

There was no more rhythm then, no control.

Just the staggering *feeling* of it all, the delectable friction, the magnificent ache, and then... *bliss.*

"*Goddamnit,*" Isaiah growled, his hips surging up to lock with mine as he came a few seconds later, with me already slumped, exhausted, onto his shoulder.

"*Ditto,*" I murmured, already half-asleep as he laughed, reaching for the fixture to turn the shower off since it was finally running cold.

I didn't protest it when he raised me off of him to change my position and then started fussing at me about the redness of my knees.

"It was worth it," I insisted, when I was tired of listening, then climbed up from his lap. I stuck my tongue out at him and then turned the shower back on, hitting him with the spray until he fought his way back up, laughing.

Definitely worth it.

My knees were *fine*, already back to their usual color by the time we actually left the bathroom. I threw on a robe, since I had no plans to go anywhere just yet, but Isaiah really *was* due back at the center, so he put on clothes.

"Hey…" he started, coming to a very sudden halt to his progress with getting ready to go. "So… there's something I need you to do for me."

I had a cheese cube ready to pop in my mouth—post orgasm snack—but I stopped, raising an eyebrow over the gravity in his tone. "Anything. What is it?"

He smirked. "Damn. You agree *first*, and then ask what it is?"

"*Zay.*"

"Okay. I… kinda punked out, with reaching out to my family. Instead of just calling or whatever… I just sent a message, with my contact info. For them to reach out if they wanted."

I frowned. "How is that punking out? You reached out first."

"Yeah, with a three line message," he shrugged. "Because I didn't want to be caught on the phone or like… a video call with people who weren't even… interested."

I put a hand to my chest, but restrained myself from the *awwww* I really wanted to let out. Instead, I said nothing, and let him continue.

"But… they… *are* interested. They reached out—my mother's sister, in Ethiopia. My aunt. And I've got cousins. They want to do a video call, so they can see me, and I can see them."

A huge smile spread over my face. "Zay, that's *amazing.* When are you doing it?"

"We scheduled it for tomorrow," he answered. "And... I want you there with me. Sorry to spring it last minute, I know you're trying to finish—"

"Fuck this *book*," I laughed. "Of course I'll be on the call with you. Thank you for inviting me."

His brow furrowed. "*Thank you for inviting me?* Nah... you're... my family. *Thank you* for agreeing to it, cause I... I can't imagine you not being there. You can't clown me if I get emotional though."

"Whaatt?" I laughed, standing to meet him at the foot of the bed. "You? Emotional? I can't even *imagine* that," I teased, reaching up to hook my arms around his shoulders. "I... am *so* happy for you. How do you feel? Are you excited?"

"I am," he admitted. "And... nervous. But mostly just... settled, if that makes sense. Like all these elements, all these moving parts are finally falling into place. Like I'm finally really *rooted*. I've got... *hobbies*, and I've got my lady, and I've got... just, a life. Remember when all this stuff, everything that's happening for us now... it was all just fantasies?"

I nodded. "Yeah. I do."

"This is... terrifying," he laughed. "I'm not supposed to be scared of shit, I know, but... this is a lot."

I giggled. "Yeah, it is, but... we can handle it," I told him, even though I had my own doubts.

"We can," he agreed, meeting my gaze with... *something* in his gaze I couldn't figure out. "I've gotta go. I'm coaching this time, instead of running around trying to keep up with youngins as referee."

I smiled. "You and your kids. I love it. Gone on, daddy Isaiah, I'll see you later."

He groaned, reaching down to grip my ass. "I kinda like how that sounds..."

"*Gone*," I laughed, pushing him away so he could finish getting ready.

Once he'd kissed me goodbye, I was able to sit back and really reflect on what he'd said. I was feeling much the same as he was... rooted.

Only I was still worried they were shallow.

So much of what we'd thought was impossible had come to fruition, and as much as I wanted to just bask in it all, something was holding me back.

And really... I'd tried to manage that feeling on my own, and then with my therapist, enough.

Instead of going back to my computer, I got up and got dressed.

I *was* going out.

To talk to the person who probably had the *most* insight on finally coming to this place of being... *settled.*

My sister.

––––––––

"DON'T JUST STARE at me. *Say something,*" I insisted, jabbing Alicia in the thigh.

When she still said nothing, I looked to Loren, who'd already been at the compound when I arrived, and insisted on being part of the conversation.

Which was fine.

She was practically family too.

"Good for you," were Loren's words, after she'd side-eyed Alicia for still sitting there, stunned. "You know, it took Alicia a long ass time to get to this point of like... just being normal. Mostly normal. She still gives killer vibes sometimes."

"I'm a bodyguard," Alicia stammered, finally speaking up. "It's literally my job—I *have* to look like I might kill a motherfucker."

"Duh bitch, but I'm saying I thought you might kill *me.* You were scary."

"And yet, you still tried to get my panties," Alicia countered.

"Correction—I was trying to get you take *my* panties. The aggressive femme vibe was strong with you, and I was horny and pregnant. *Excuse me* for wanting the strap, damn."

"Can we focus on *my* problem right now?" I interrupted. If I didn't already know this entire story, maybe I'd be tuned in, but right now I needed help."

Alicia looked to me, staring for a long moment before her lips turned up in a smile. "You don't *have* a problem, little sister. Well… let me rephrase—this is just the dilemma for people like us. Do you think I'm not always concerned something might go wrong?"

"You are?"

"I hired a secret protection detail for you, Dosh. You tell me," she laughed. "In seriousness, though… you just need time. Isaiah coming back into your life is a big change, and it's only been… what, like two months? You've *just* popped the cork on this thing—it's gotta have time to breathe."

I sighed. "Fine. I get that. But this feeling… this anxiety, and paranoia… it *can't* be normal! Like, it's literally making me sick."

"That's too much, baby girl," Loren chimed, sipping from her wine. "Speaking of popping corks… is that nigga not popping yours? That's a great way to relax."

"We've been doing it *so much*," I laughed, shaking my head. "He came to my place smelling like skunks earlier, and I still wanted him. And I'm *still* stressed. And still horny," I said, crossing my arms over my sore breasts. Sex couldn't be the problem when I was sitting here *aching* to be touched again already."

Loren put her glass down, eyebrow raised. "Hmm. Hunching like rabbits. Stressed. Sick. Sensitive to smell…. Girl, you're pregnant."

Alicia about choked on *her* wine as I shook my head.

"That's not even possible."

"Says who?" Loren inquired. "You're talking about that tubal they did on y'all? Alicia is getting hers reversed."

"What?!" Alicia and I exclaimed, at the same time—maybe for different reasons.

"I haven't decided on that yet, and we don't even know for sure!"

"Which is why we're speaking it into the atmosphere," Loren shrugged. "For all we know, it could've reversed *itself*, if they just tied them instead of more severe methods. Y'all were young. It happens."

"But... I... *what?*" I said, my heart racing now. "I thought it was... *permanent*. Like... *permanent*."

Loren smirked. "Maybe it is, maybe it isn't," she replied. "I'm just saying that it's really not *impossible* that you're pregnant." She shook her head. "You young girls always think you just won't get pregnant cause you *think so*. I had a client who had her period timed down to the *hour* it was gonna start. Guess what? *Pregnant*. Cause she was fucking. Like you were fucking. Raw."

"This isn't *funny*," I whined, and Loren laughed.

"I'm not being *funny*. I'm serious. Are all of y'all really just operating like pregnancy isn't even *possible?*" Loren asked. "That's the problem, right there. Have you missed a period?"

"*No.*" I immediately countered. "I mean... not... not really? It was... kinda light."

"Implantation bleeding, my dear," Loren said, then sipped.

"You need to take a test," Alicia said, finally speaking again. "It's the only way to really know."

"I'm *not* pregnant."

"Because you said so. Right. That's super scientific," Loren giggled, then stood. "Come on, let's go get a test. You're driving, since you're the sober one."

I looked to Alicia, wanting her to be the voice of reason, but instead... she drained the rest of her wine glass, and stood. "Come on."

IT WAS A SHORT TRIP.

There was a convenience store just up the block, and Loren volunteered to go in. She came back with a bag filled with several tests and a water bottle she made me guzzle on the way back, just in case.

Thirty minutes after she first introduced the possibility...

It was confirmed.

Pregnant.

"What the *fuck* am I supposed to do with this?" I asked out loud, staring at the two pink lines confirming the positive. I looked up, looking between Alicia and Loren, wanting one of them to tell me what to do.

"Well... you've got options," Loren said, taking a pragmatic approach. "Nothing says you have to keep the pregnancy. *And* ... it's worth mentioning that a positive test doesn't mean its viable. A tubal raises the risks of ectopic pregnancy, so we should probably get you into the office real soon, so we can see what's happening."

My eyes went wide. "Ectopic... what is that?"

"It means the egg implanted somewhere it can't actually grow," Loren explained. "And if that's the case, it's a pretty dangerous thing for you, that will need to be immediately taken care of. So it's great that we'll have caught it early."

I shook my head, pressing a hand to my stomach. "But it's not that. I don't... want it to be that."

Alicia raised an eyebrow. "So... you *want* to be pregnant? You want a baby?"

"I... don't know," I sighed. "Can anybody want something they didn't believe was possible?"

"That's the story of our lives," Alicia reminded me. "Wanting the impossible. And look at all these other *"impossible"* things that you've grabbed onto."

I let out another breath. "You're right, but this is... *wow.*"

Before anyone else could say anything else, our quiet was interrupted by noise.

Familiar male voices mixed in with the youthful soprano of a child.

Cree coming in, with Yaya in tow, and Pen, who was supposed to be dropping Yaya off from their girls' day... and Isaiah.

They stopped at the door to the living room, their expressions concerned as they looked around at us, probably wondering why the energy was so serious.

"Mommy, you took a temp-uh-cha?" Yaya asked, and my eyes went big, realizing she thought the pregnancy test—perched on top of the box, on the coffee table—was a thermometer.

"Uh... yeah, sure," Loren said, snatching the box and test up, but there was no way the guys hadn't already seen it.

So...

Okay.

Cool.

"I'm pregnant," I blurted, looking Isaiah right in the face, watching intently for his reaction. At first his lips just parted, brow furrowed, confused.

And he just... stood there, gaping.

But then he looked at Cree, who gave a subtle shake of his head.

I had no idea what that was about, but the next thing off Isaiah's lips was, "Marry me."

And... then it was just me and him, nothing else.

"*What?*" I asked, half-confused. Vaguely, I registered Cree muttering something about *told his ass not to do it without a ring,* and Penelope screeching "WHAT, OH MY GOD!" but... I was focused, really.

"It's abrupt. I know," he said, dropping the bag that had been hooked over his shoulder to approach me as I stood from my seat on the couch. "But... I've been thinking about it— scared about it... since the day you caught me following you. I love you, Dee. And if you're... having my baby, which is nuts, but we'll come back to that... I want it all. I want it official. So... yeah... *marry me*."

"I... *yes*," I nodded, through very sudden tears, as everything came rushing back into reality.

Isaiah kissing me, Yaya yelling, excited even though she didn't know why, the others all chattering. When he let me go, the first place I turned was to Alicia. In the back of my mind, I expected her to be frowning, disapproving.

I wasn't expecting crying.

I wasn't expecting her to throw her arms around me, hugging me tight around the neck as she whispered – genuinely, *happily* – "*Congratulations.*" And then Penelope was on us too, squealing. They were practically suffocating me, and Zay was complaining about not being able to get to his baby mama. Cree was still fussing about him proposing without a ring, and Loren was laughing at it all and tipsy dialing Tempest so she could be in on it.

And it was all very loud and overwhelming... but that was okay.

It was more than okay, it was... *perfect*.

And I knew right at that moment... *this* was what wholeness felt like.

Finally.

THE END.

EXTRAS

If you enjoyed Dacia's story, please consider leaving a review!

For more information - relevant videos from my youtube channel, my Pinterest board with images that inspired the book, as well as links to other books that give more context for the world presented here - you can visit The Unbroken Rose page on my website!

ABOUT THE AUTHOR

Christina C. Jones is a best selling romance novelist and digital media creator.

A timeless storyteller, she is lauded by readers for her ability to seamlessly weave the complexities of modern life into captivating tales of black romance.

As an author, Christina's work has been featured in various media outlets such as Write 2 Be Magazine and Book Riot, and is the winner of numerous community awards.

In addition to her full-time writing career, she cofounded Girl, Have You Read - a popular digital platform that amplifies black romance authors and their stories.

A former graphic designer, Christina has a passion for making things beautiful and can usually be found crafting and cooking in her spare time.

She currently lives in Arkansas with her husband and their two children.

To learn more, visit www.beingmrsjones.com.

OTHER TITLES BY CHRISTINA JONES:

For direct links and more information, you can visit my website.

Wonder (Post-Apocalyptic)

Love and Other Things

Eternally Tethered
Haunted (paranormal)
Coveted

Mine Tonight (erotica)

The Love Sisters
I Think I Might Love You
I Think I Might Need You
I Think I Might Want You

Sugar Valley
The Culmination Of Everything
The Point Of It All

Equilibrium
Love Notes
Grow Something
In Tandem
Bittersweet
Plus One

Press Rewind

Frosted.Whipped.Buttered.

Five Start Enterprises

Anonymous Acts

More Than a Hashtag

Relationship Goals

High Stakes

Ante Up

King of Hearts

Deuces Wild

Sweet Heat

Hints of Spice (Highlight Reel spinoff)

A Dash of Heat

A Touch of Sugar

Truth, Lies, and Consequences

The Truth – His Side, Her Side, And the Truth About Falling
In Love

The Lies – The Lies We Tell About Life, Love, and Everything in
Between

Friends & Lovers:

Finding Forever

Chasing Commitment

Strictly Professional:

Strictly Professional

Unfinished Business

Made in the USA
Coppell, TX
27 January 2022

72500402R00095